Marco Balzano

I'm Staying Here

Translated from the Italian
by Jill Foulston

Other Press
New York

Library of Congress Cataloging-in-Publication Data

Names: Balzano, Marco, author. | Foulston, Jill, translator.
Title: I'm staying here / Marco Balzano ; translated from the Italian by Jill Foulston.
Other titles: Resto qui. English | I am staying here
Description: New York : Other Press, [2020] | "Originally published as
Resto qui in 2018 by Giulio Einaudi editore. First published in English in 2020
by Head of Zeus Ltd"—Title page verso.
Identifiers: LCCN 2020012687 (print) | LCCN 2020012688 (ebook) |
ISBN 9781635420371 (paperback ; acid-free paper) | ISBN 9781635420388 (ebook)
Subjects: LCSH: World War, 1939-1945—Austria—Tyrol—Fiction. |
Floods—Austria—Tyrol—Fiction. | Tyrol (Austria)—Fiction.
Classification: LCC PQ4902.A528 R4713 2020 (print) |
LCC PQ4902.A528 (ebook) | DDC 853/.92—dc23
LC record available at https://lccn.loc.gov/2020012687
LC ebook record available at https://lccn.loc.gov/2020012688

I'm
Staying
Here

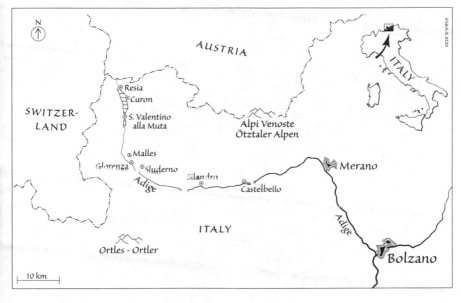

Map of the South Tyrol

Part One

The Years

1

You don't know a thing about me, but then again, as my daughter, you know a lot. The smell of your skin, the warmth of your breath, your twitchy nerves; I gave them all to you. So I'm going to talk to you as if you'd looked into my heart.

I could describe you down to the last detail. Actually, some mornings, when the snow is high and the house is wrapped in a silence that takes your breath away, new details come to mind. A few weeks ago I remembered a little mole you had on your shoulder. You'd always point it out whenever I bathed you in the tub; you were obsessed with it. Or that curl behind your ear, the only one in that honey-colored hair of yours.

I'm wary of taking out the few photos I've kept. Tears come more easily as you age, and I hate crying. I hate it because it's idiotic, and because it's no consolation. All it does is exhaust me, and then I don't want to eat anything or put on my nightshirt before getting into bed. But you have to look after yourself, clench your fists even when the skin on them is covered in spots. Try to let things go. That's what your father taught me.

★

All these years, I've imagined myself a good mother. Reliable, lively, friendly… adjectives that don't really fit me. In the village, they still call me Teacher, but they greet me from a distance. They know I'm not that sociable. Sometimes I remember a game I used to play with the children in year one: "Draw the animal that looks most like you." These days I'd draw a tortoise with its head in its shell.

I like to imagine that I wasn't one of those meddling mothers. I would never ask you, as my mother always did, who this or that person was, if you had time for him or wanted to go out with him. But maybe it's just another one of those stories I tell myself, and if I had you with me, I'd bombard you with questions, looking at you from the corner of my eye every time you were evasive. As the years go by, you feel less superior to your parents. If I make comparisons now, I come out worse overall. Your grandmother was harsh and difficult. She knew what she thought about everything, had no trouble telling black from white and no problem being blunt. I, on the other hand, got lost in all the shades of gray. According to her, my studies were to blame. She thought anyone who was educated was unnecessarily difficult. An idler, a know-it-all, a hair-splitter. But I believed that the greatest knowledge lay in words, especially for a woman. Facts, stories, fantasies… what mattered was being hungry for them and keeping them close for times when life got complicated or bleak. I believed that words could save me.

2

I've never cared much for men. The idea that they were connected with love seemed ridiculous to me. As far as I was concerned, they were too clumsy, hairy or boorish, sometimes all three at once. Around here, everyone had a bit of land and a few animals, and that's the smell they carried around with them – of sweat and stables, If I had to imagine making love, I preferred to think about a woman. Better the sharp cheekbones of a girl than a man's prickly skin. But best of all was to stay single, accountable to no one. Actually, I wouldn't have minded becoming a nun. I was more excited about the idea of removing myself from the world than having a family. But it's always been difficult to think about God. Whenever I thought about him I got confused.

Erich was the only one I ever looked at. I'd see him go by at dawn, his hat pulled over his forehead, his cigarette already hanging from the side of his mouth at that hour. Each time, I wanted to go to the window to say hello, but if I'd opened it Ma would have been cold and she'd surely have shouted at me to close it immediately.

"Trina, are you crazy?" she'd have shrieked.

Ma was always yelling. And in any case, even if I'd opened the window, what would I have said to him? At seventeen, I was so awkward that at best I'd have stammered. So I just stayed there, watching him walk toward the woods, while Grau, his spotted dog, drove the flock on. When he was with the cows, Erich dragged himself around so slowly that he hardly seemed to move at all. So I'd bend my head over my books, sure that I'd see him in the same place. When I raised it he looked tiny at the end of the road, under larches that are no longer there.

That spring, I found myself thinking of Erich more and more often, my books open and a pencil in my mouth. When Ma wasn't bustling about two feet away, I'd ask Pa if the farmer's life was one for dreamers. After hoeing the garden, you can go to the fields with your animals, sit down on a rock and stay there in peace and quiet, watching a river that has been flowing peacefully for who knows how many centuries, and a cold and infinite sky...

"Farmers can do all that, can't they, Pa?"

Pa chuckled, his pipe between his teeth. "Go and ask the boy you watch from your window every morning if his is the work of a dreamer..."

The first time I talked to him he was in the farmyard. Pa worked as a carpenter in Resia, but even our home seemed like his workshop. People were always coming and going, asking him to repair something. When the visitors left, Ma grumbled that we never had any peace. And he, unable to put up with the least criticism, would tell her there was nothing to grumble about, since a craftsman is working even when he's offering someone a drink or stopping for a chat; that's how he builds his clientele. To cut the discussion short, she'd tweak his nose, that spongy nose of his.

"It's grown bigger," she'd say.

"So has your arse!"

Ma would lose her temper. "Look who I married, a real lowlife!" and she'd toss the tea towel at him. Pa would smirk and throw his pencil at her. Another rag from her, another pencil from him. Throwing things was their way of loving each other.

That afternoon, Erich and Pa stood smoking, their eyes wide as they watched the clouds falling over the Ortler Alps. Pa told him to wait for a moment while he went to fetch a glass of grappa. Erich wasn't much of a talker; he'd lift his chin with a faint smile and a confidence that made me feel small.

"What are you going to do after you finish school? Teach?" he asked me.

"Maybe, yes. Or I might go somewhere far away," I answered, trying to sound like an adult.

As soon as I said that his face darkened. He pulled so hard on his cigarette the ash nearly burned his fingers.

"I never want to leave Curon," he said, gesturing toward the valley.

I looked at him like a child who's run out of words, and Erich caressed my cheek as he left.

"Tell your father I'll have a grappa with him some other day."

I nodded, unsure what else to say. I sat there, my elbows on the table, watching him go. Every now and again I'd glance over at the door, afraid that Ma would suddenly appear. Sometimes love makes you feel like a thief.

3

In the spring of '23 I was studying for my high school diploma. Mussolini had waited until the moment I was taking my diploma to shake up the schools. The year before, the fascists had marched on Bolzano, subjecting the city to a violent occupation. They burned the public buildings, beat people, drove the burgomaster out by force. And as usual, the *carabinieri* stood there watching. If they hadn't folded their arms, just like the king had the year before, fascism would never have survived. Even today, I find it unsettling to walk through Bolzano. Everything seems hostile to me. There are so many signs of the twenty-year fascist regime, and seeing them again makes me think of Erich. How angry he'd be!

Until that time, life had kept pace with the rhythm of the seasons, especially in these border valleys. Like an echo that fades away, history seemed never to have reached them. Our language was German, our religion Christianity, our work was in fields and cowsheds. Nothing more was needed to understand this mountain people, to whom you also belong, if for no other reason than that you were born here.

Mussolini renamed streets, streams, mountains... those assassins even molested the dead, changing inscriptions on tombstones. They Italianized our names, replaced shop signs. We were forbidden to wear our traditional clothes. Overnight, we ended up with teachers from the Veneto, Lombardy and Sicily. They didn't understand us and we didn't understand them. Here in the South Tyrol, Italian was an exotic language, something you heard on the gramophone or when a salesman from Vallarsa came up the Trentino on his way to do business in Austria.

Your rather unusual name immediately imprinted itself on people's minds, but for those who couldn't remember it you were always Erich and Trina's daughter. They said we were two peas in a pod.

"If she gets lost, someone will take her home!" the baker muttered, and he'd greet you by pulling faces with his tooth-less mouth. Remember? Whenever you smelled bread in the street, you'd drag me by the hand to buy you some. There was nothing you liked better than warm bread.

I knew everyone who lived in Curon, but I had only two friends, Maja and Barbara. They don't live here anymore. They left years ago and I don't even know if they're still alive. We were such close friends that we went to the same school. We couldn't go to the teachers' training school because it was too far away, but it was a great adventure going to Bolzano to take the annual exams. We roamed the city excitedly, finally seeing the world beyond the mountain and the pastures: apartment buildings, shops, busy streets.

Maja and I had a real vocation to teach and we couldn't wait to get inside a classroom. Barbara would have preferred to be a seamstress. She enrolled with us because "that way," she said, "we can spend more time together." Back then, she was my shadow. We spent our time accompanying one another home. At the farmyard gate, one of us would say to the other, "Look, it's still light, I'll go home with you."

We took long walks, skirting the river or the edge of the wood, and during those walks, I remember Barbara was always saying, "If only I had your personality…"

"But why? What am I like?"

"Well, you're clear-headed and you know where you're going, whereas I get confused about everything and I'm always looking for someone to hold my hand."

"I don't feel being like me is so great."

"You only say that because you're so hard to please."

I shrugged my shoulders. "Well, I'd give my personality any day to be pretty like you."

She'd smile then, and if there wasn't anyone around, or if the sky was getting dark, she'd kiss me and say sweet things that I no longer remember.

With the Duce's arrival, we realized that we were in danger of not finding jobs since we weren't Italian. So all three of us settled down to study Italian in the hope that they'd hire us anyway.

That spring, we spent our afternoons by the lake with grammar books. We'd see each other after lunch, and one of us would arrive with some fruit in a napkin, another with her mouth full.

"No German for now!" I'd say, to call them to order.

Maja would protest, slapping a notebook full of her doodling. "I wanted to become a teacher, but not in someone else's language!"

"What about me? I wanted to be a dress designer!" Barbara said.

"Look, it's hardly on doctor's orders that you're studying to become a teacher," Maja retorted.

"My, my, listen to this witch... What do you mean, it's not doctor's orders?" Barbara protested, putting her red hair, which was always getting in her way, into a ponytail. Then she'd start telling us again that we had to go off and live together, and not get married.

"Listen: if we get married we'll turn into slaves!"

When I got back home I'd go to bed immediately. I was always hungry for solitude. I'd crawl into bed and stay in the damp and dark of my room, thinking. I knew that whether I liked it or not, I was growing up and it troubled me. I don't know if you have ever been afraid like this, or whether you're more like your father, who saw life like a river. Me? Whenever I got close to any sort of change or goal, whether my diploma or marriage, I promptly felt like running away and throwing it all up in the air. Why do we have to keep moving forward in life? Even when you were born, I thought, "Why can't I keep her inside me a little longer?"

*

That May, Maja, Barbara and I saw each other during the week, too, not just every once in a while, or at Mass on Sundays. We practiced that strange language, hoping that the fascists would appreciate our application and our diplomas. But since deep down we didn't believe it ourselves, rather than studying grammar we often sat in a circle and listened to Italian songs on Barbara's records.

> A kiss you'll get
> If you come back
> But there'll be no more
> If you leave for war

A week before our written exams Pa gave me permission to sleep over at Barbara's. It took some doing, but in the end I managed it.

"Very well, child. You can go to your friend's but you'll have to bring me a perfect report card."

"And what do you consider a perfect report card?" I asked, kissing him on the cheek.

"Well, one with an average of ten!" he said, hands spread. And Ma, who was sitting beside him darning socks, nodded. Ma took advantage of every spare minute to darn socks, since "if your feet are cold, you're cold all over," she'd say.

As it happens, I didn't get top marks. It was Maja who paid for drinks and made the tart, as we'd agreed when school started. In Barbara's view, Maja had only got a ten because her professor was a lech who was always ogling her breasts.

"I got a seven because of these two crab apples," she protested, thrusting her breasts forward and weighing them in her hands.

"You got a seven because you're a dunce," Maja retorted. Barbara quickly grabbed her and they rolled over the grass. Squinting in the sun, I laughed as I watched them.

4

Once we'd graduated, we found ourselves back beside the lake, beneath the larches. But there was no more talk about studying Italian.

"If they hire us at the school, great. If not, to hell with them!" Maja declared.

"No one around here has a diploma. They'll have to take us," Barbara said.

"Don't imagine that that piece of paper means anything to the fascists! They want to give work to Italians."

"We'll end up having studied for nothing," Maja sighed. "I'll have to go and work in the shop with my father and we'll do nothing but argue."

"Definitely better than staying at home mending socks," I said, feeling suffocated at the mere thought of spending my days with Ma.

Meanwhile, the fascists occupied not only schools but town halls, post offices and the courts. Employees from the Tyrol were dismissed on the spot and the Italians hung up signs in their offices saying IT IS FORBIDDEN TO SPEAK GERMAN and MUSSOLINI IS ALWAYS RIGHT. They imposed curfews,

Saturday afternoon rallies when the *podestà* appeared, and obligatory holidays.

Maja would say, "I feel like I'm walking over a minefield." She quickly tired of our chats, which always ended up on trivial subjects. "But don't you see what the hell is happening?" she exclaimed in annoyance. "Curon, Resia, San Valentino… since the fascists arrived, nothing is ours anymore. The men don't go to the inn, the women hug the walls when they walk, there's not a soul about in the evening! How can you let it all slide off you?"

"My brother says fascism's days are numbered," Barbara replied, trying to calm her.

But Maja would not be calmed. She snorted like a horse and lay back on the grass, saying we were just conceited.

She'd had a different upbringing from ours. Her father was an educated man who spent hours explaining to his children what was going on in the South Tyrol and the rest of the world. He'd tell them who this governor was, or that minister. Whenever Barbara and I were in the house as well he'd embark on long discourses, rattling off a string of names and places we'd never heard of. He'd finish with a warning: "When you get married, tell your husbands, and remember it yourselves: If you don't get involved with politics, politics will get involved with you!" And he'd retreat to the other room. Maja adored her father and as soon as he finished speaking, she'd nod her head in obedience. Barbara and I would look out of the window feeling dumb as goats.

"At this rate Maja is going to become more fanatical than her father," Barbara said on the way home.

Sometimes Barbara and I went out on our own. We'd get on our bicycles and go as far as San Valentino, riding along the lake to feel the cool of the water clinging to our sweaty faces.

"It seems like the mountains are growing along with us," she said, pedaling along, her chin in the air.

"Do you think they're hiding the world from us?" I asked. Some days I felt like running away and others, like shutting myself up in the house.

"What do you care about the world?" she laughed.

When he came home from the shop, Pa would say that outside there was a whiff of war in the air. Maja's parents said that it would be better to leave for Austria, to get away from the fascists. Barbara's parents wanted to join their relatives in Germany.

In the meantime, the population of the South Tyrol was also changing. The months went by and colonies of Italians continued to arrive, sent by the Duce. Some even came here to Curon. I immediately recognized those strangers from the south, suitcases in hand and noses in the air, looking at mountain slopes they'd never seen, clouds that were too low.

It was us against them from the start. One language against another. People who laid claim to age-old roots against the authority of newfound power.

★

17

Erich often came by the house. He'd always been friends with Pa, and Pa loved him because he was an orphan.

Ma, though, didn't like him all that much. "That kid is uppity," she said. "It's as if he's doing you a favor by speaking to you." She expected from others the warmth she herself lacked.

Pa would invite him to sit on the stool, and then he'd turn his seat around and lean his elbows on the back, resting his whiskery cheeks in his hands. Erich was like a son to him. An anxious son who asked advice about everything. I'd spy on them from behind the door frame. I held my breath, trying to make myself thin, and flattened my palms against the wall. If my brother, Peppi, appeared, I'd put him beside me and cover his mouth. He'd try to wriggle away but in those days I could keep him still. Peppi was seven years younger than me, and I didn't know what to say about him other than that he was a mummy's boy. He was just a brat with a dirty face and skinned knees.

"It seems that the Italian government wants to get the dam project going again," Erich announced one evening. "Some of the farmers who take their animals to San Valentino saw work crews arriving."

Pa shrugged. "They've been saying that for years, but then nothing happens," he replied with a good-natured smile.

"If they are going to build it, we have to find a way to stop them," Erich went on, looking somewhere else. "The fascists have every reason to ruin us and scatter us throughout Italy."

"Don't worry. Even if fascism lasts, it's impossible to build a dam here. The ground is too muddy."

But Erich's gray eyes remained as troubled as a cat's.

The dam had been announced for the first time in 1911. Developers from the firm of Montecatini wanted to drive out the residents of Resia and Curon and take advantage of the river's current to produce energy. Italian industrialists and politicians claimed that the Alto Adige was a mine of white gold, and they sent engineers with increasing frequency to inspect the valleys and survey the rivers' courses. Our villages would disappear in a watery grave. The farms, church, workshops and the pastures; they'd all be submerged. If there were a dam, we'd lose our houses, our animals, our work. If there were a dam, nothing would remain of us. We would have to emigrate, become something else. Find another way of earning our bread, another place, become another people. We would die a long way from the Venosta Valley and the Tyrol.

In 1911, the project didn't proceed because the land was considered unstable. Composed only of dolomite debris, it lacked substance. Now that the Duce was in power, the plan was to build industrial centers in Bolzano and Merano. The cities would double or triple in size, with Italians coming in droves looking for work – and everyone knew that the demand for energy would increase enormously.

Down at the inn, in the churchyard, in Pa's workshop, Erich

made himself hoarse. "They'll come back, you know. You can be sure that they'll return." But while he got worked up over it, the peasants kept drinking, smoking, shuffling cards. They dismissed any discussion, pursing their lips or waving their hands in the air, as if to catch flies.

"If they can't see it, it doesn't exist," Erich told Pa. "Give them a glass of wine and they stop thinking."

5

Instead of hiring us, they chose semi-illiterates from Sicily and the countryside around Venice. In any case, that Tyrolean children should learn something was the least of the Duce's concerns.

We three spent our days walking dejectedly through the crowded piazza, the street vendors shouting into the evening and women clustered around their carts.

One morning we ran into the priest, who pulled us into an empty alleyway with moss-stained walls. He said that if we really wanted to teach, we'd have to go to the catacombs. Going to the catacombs meant teaching secretly. It was illegal and could mean fines, beatings, castor oil. You could end up being transported to some remote island. Barbara immediately said no. Maja and I looked at each other hesitantly.

"There's no time for reflection!" the priest urged us.

When I mentioned it at home, Ma started shouting that I'd end up in Sicily with all the black people. But Pa said that I was doing the right thing. I wasn't particularly keen; I've never been especially courageous. I went so I'd look good to Erich. I'd heard him talk about going to secret meetings, getting hold of German newspapers, and belonging to a club that favored German annexation of the South Tyrol. Teaching in the cata-combs seemed like a good way of making an impression on him, but also a way of finding out if the reality of teaching matched up to my idea of it.

The priest assigned me to a cellar in San Valentino, and Maja to a stable in Resia. I'd go at around five in the after-noon, when it was already dark. Or on Sunday before Mass, always in the dark. I cycled, out of breath, down dirt roads I never knew existed. If a leaf shivered or a cricket chirruped, I wanted to cry out. I would leave the bike behind a bush on the outskirts of the village and walk head down so as not to bump into any *carabinieri*. At the time, it seemed like there were more of those damned *carabinieri* than there were moths. I saw them everywhere.

In Signora Marta's cellar, we piled up the wooden barrels and old furniture and sat on heaps of straw. We whispered because we had to listen for sounds from outside. A few steps in the courtyard were enough to frighten us. The little boys were less responsive than the little girls, who looked at me with fear in their eyes. There were seven of them and I taught them to read and write. I'd take their hands and enclose them within mine, like a shell. I'd guide them as they drew the letters of the alphabet, words, their first sentences. In the beginning, it seemed an impossible task, but as the evenings continued, one by one they began to read, pronouncing each syllable, using a finger to keep their place. It was wonderful teaching German. I liked it so much that sometimes I forgot

I was a secret teacher. I thought about Erich, and how proud he'd be to see me down there, writing numbers and letters on a slate for the children to copy and repeat together in hushed voices. On the way home, I'd let my hair down to get rid of my headache. But the headache was good company. It distracted me from fear.

One evening two *carabinieri* broke down the cellar door as if we were bandits. One little girl started screaming, and the other children scattered, turning to the wall so they would not have to look. Only Sepp stayed in his place. Slowly he approached one of the *carabinieri*, and I'll never forget the cold rage with which he insulted him. The *carabiniere* didn't understand German but he gave him a slap in the face. The child didn't move an inch. He didn't cry. He never stopped staring at him with hatred.

When the children had left the room, the *carabinieri* smashed the slate against a wall, kicked in the barrels, tipped over the furniture.

"We'll throw you in prison!" they yelled, dragging me to the town hall.

They left me locked up all night in a bare room. On the wall was a photo of Mussolini, hands on hips, looking proud. They said he was much loved by women, and I tried to understand what was so great about him. The moment I dozed off, a *carabiniere* would come in and beat his baton on the table to wake me up. He'd shine a lamp in my face and over and over he'd ask, "Who gives you the materials? Where are the other secret teachers hiding? Whose children are these?"

When Pa came to get me, they ripped out his mustache, as they did with anyone who displeased them. They made him hand over a lot of money. I felt like something the cat had dragged in, with stomach cramps and bloodshot eyes. I thought Pa would forbid me to go back, but at the fountain, he wiped my face with a wet cloth and said, "You just have to keep on going."

We changed our location. We moved into the attic of one of Pa's clients. All of the students came back, except for the little girl who'd started screaming. The students rarely had any paper; sometimes they tore a page out of the notebook used in the Italian school, which they were obliged to attend. The lesson over, I'd let them out the back. Once there was an unexpected knock on the door. Quick as mice, we climbed up onto the roof. I kept the children close to me, afraid they'd fall – and then the owner came up, laughing: it was the baker delivering bread.

It was easier in the summer. We had our lessons in the fields and the sun and the light chased away dark thoughts. Outdoors, disguising our secret school was like a game. We spent hours trying out a performance I wanted to put on at Maja's farm for Christmas. We read aloud, stories by Hans Christian Andersen and the Brothers Grimm, but also forbidden poems, which I'd learned by heart as a child in the

Austrian school. Every now and again a sound from the street would shut me up, and then Sepp would take my hand and reassure me with his ice-blue eyes. Years later, I heard that Sepp had become one of the youngest Nazi collaborators, selecting prisoners in Bolzano's concentration camp.

Every night, I dreamed of *carabinieri* and Blackshirts. I'd wake up with a start, bathed in sweat, and then lie awake for hours staring at the ceiling. Before I went back to sleep, I'd search the farmhouse to make sure there really weren't any hidden inside. I even looked under the bed and in the wardrobe, and Ma, who slept lightly, would call from the other room, "Trina, what are you doing up at this hour?"

"Checking to make sure there aren't any *carabinieri!*"

"Under the bed?!"

"Well…"

I'd hear her turn over, mumbling that I was half mad.

All this time, the secret schools were growing in number. The smugglers brought us notebooks from Bavaria and Austria, abacuses, slates. They left everything with the priests, who allocated the materials to us. Despite putting up signs everywhere that read IT IS FORBIDDEN TO SPEAK GERMAN, the fascists didn't succeed in Italianizing anything, and they became increasingly violent.

The following winter, the children started disguising themselves to fool the *carabinieri*. They'd come bundled in coats as if they were feverish, or in work outfits hastily cobbled together, or spruced up as if for their first communion… When I cycled home in the evening and my house finally appeared, the kerosene lamp glowing behind smoky windows, I'd laugh at having got away with it one more time.

One day I went out with Barbara. We kissed each other, lying on the grass, and when we got up we noticed that our clothes were torn. We liked kissing but I couldn't say why. Maybe you don't need a reason when you're young. We sat on a tree trunk. Barbara had some chocolate biscuits wrapped up in paper.

"I like teaching in German," I told her, my mouth full, "and I like it even more, since it's acting against the fascists."

"But aren't you afraid?"

"I was at the beginning. Now I've learned to observe the children's faces. When they're calm, I become calm too."

"Those bastards haven't let us teach one single day," she said, disheartened.

"Why don't you join us?"

"Trina, I've told you: I don't have your personality. I'd have died of a heart attack if I'd gone through what you did."

"It was just a nasty scare."

"I'm helping out in the shop now. My father is counting on me," she went on evasively.

"But you can teach without stopping work! You give lessons when you have a few free hours," I finished hurriedly. "You'll see, it'll do you good to be with the children. They're so much better than adults."

She thought about it for a while, chewing her lip. And then: "Well, okay, but don't tell anyone. Not even my parents."

The priest agreed as soon as I told him about her. There was a group ready to start in Resia.

Barbara barely had time to tell me that she was enjoying herself and that she liked the teaching. It was a Thursday evening, and it was raining in Curon, the usual slanting November rain. I was at home making meatballs with Peppi.

Someone let their bicycle fall outside, pounded on the door, tried to get in.

"They went down and cleared out the sacristy, broke everything and kicked the children out! Then they dragged her out by the hair and threw her in a car," cried Maja, breathless and looking grim. "They're sending her to Lipari."

I didn't even manage to ask if they'd mistreated her. I stood there on the doorstep, the saliva curdling in my mouth.

The rain kept falling, soaking my face.

6

Pa and Erich always went through the same rituals. The small talk, the grappa, cigarettes. So did I. I'd take my place behind the door frame, indulging in daydreams, and then run into the kitchen as soon as he got up to go home. Each time, I pretended to be folding a tablecloth or drinking water like someone who'd escaped from the desert. I thought this could go on for ever. And deep down, I wasn't unhappy about that. Seeing him always on his own, always on his stool, made me feel I wasn't alone. Can't this be one way to love someone? Watching them from hiding, without going through the usual drama of getting married and having kids?

Then one November day he showed up with an enormous gash in his jaw, a wound that traveled from his neck and down under his shirt. It seemed that someone had tried to split his head in two like a watermelon. Pa instinctively grabbed him under the arms and took him to a chair in front of the stove.

"I've spent the last few nights hiding with a group of peasants outside of town. Some Italian inspectors arrived. 'We've been living here for centuries. Our fathers and our children live here and our dead are here!' I shouted. At which point one of those cowards took out his truncheon but an engineer stopped him and told me we could come to some agreement. He told me, 'Progress is worth more than a huddle of houses.'"

I was sad to see him disfigured, but also happy to stand beside him at last, without having to hide. I wanted to soothe him with some cotton wool, and say, Keep talking, Erich. I'll take care of you.

"One of the others shouted out that we wouldn't leave for any reason, that the entire village would resist. 'We'll get our pitchforks and open the stables, let the dogs loose!' And that's how we got lashed and beaten up." He touched his wound, as if to reassure himself that it had happened.

Pa listened, speechless.

"Do you want to stay here and eat?" I asked. Right away, Ma glared at me.

But Erich said he needed to be alone.

One afternoon I went to Barbara's house. I couldn't accept that although we lived only a hundred steps away from each other, we no longer held hands or took walks together from one day to the next. So as soon as Ma went to lie down after lunch, I took a slice of cake from the table, wrapped it in a tea towel and left the house without telling anyone.

I stood at the door of her farmhouse, sweating, unable to move, to knock or call out her name. I waited for her to put her head through the window next to the stables, like when her parents wouldn't give her permission to go out. She left it open some summer days, and I'd whistle for her as I went by. She'd whistle back and then jump down, always carrying something sweet in a cone of paper, which we'd eat as we walked along. When we whistled like that, her sister Alexandra said we were more uncouth than the shepherds.

I have no idea how long I stood in front of her door, my legs frozen, as if paralyzed. Until Alexandra came out. When she saw me she dropped the bags she was carrying to the ground.

"Can I speak to Barbara?" I asked in a faint voice.

Alexandra stared at me – whether in scorn or amazement I couldn't say – and then motioned with her chin for me to leave.

"May I speak to Barbara?" I asked again.

"She's not home."

"You're just saying that because you don't want me to talk to her."

"That's right, I don't," she said, compressing her lips. "And she doesn't either."

"Please… even from here. She only has to stick her head out for a minute."

"They're exiling her because of you. Did you know that?"

We stood there in silence, like duelists. The sheep bleated from the stables.

"Get out of my way!" I suddenly shouted. "Out of my way!"

I threw myself at her, my head lowered like a bull's, and then I shoved her, gripped by a feeling that it wasn't me deciding what to do, but some unknown part of my body. We tussled like bitches. Alexandra yanked my hair and kicked me to the ground.

"If you don't get out of here I'll call my father."

All at once, I realized what I'd done. I could have died of shame. My tears coursed down cheeks scratched by her nails.

She stood at the door, guarding it until I left. As I walked away, I wanted to turn round one more time and beg her at least to give Barbara the slice of cake I'd brought her – it had fallen to the ground near the bags. But I'd lost my voice.

I wandered around by myself, in no particular direction. It was evening by the time I got home. As soon as I stepped inside, Pa came up to me.

"Do you mind telling us where you were? It's been dark for some time, you scamp!"

My eyes were still red from crying but he was so intent on lecturing me that he hadn't noticed a thing, not even my scratches.

"Luckily for you, your mother is feverish and she went to bed early."

I apologized and swore that it would never happen again, and I was already on my way to bed when he said he had something important to tell me.

"Tomorrow, Pa. I've had a rotten day."

He put his hands on my arms and pushed me down on the stool.

"I talked to him," he began.

"To whom?"

"What do you mean, to whom?!"

"I told you, Pa, I've had an awful day. Just let me go to bed."

"He says it hadn't occurred to him, but it suits him. In fact, he's happy!"

Only in that moment did I realize that he was referring to Erich. And then I rubbed my face with my hands and dried my eyes with his handkerchief.

"But why didn't you ask me first?"

"Oh my, child, I try to help and you treat me like this? Don't you want to get married? Would you prefer to fold tablecloths all your life?"

I'd never felt so bewildered. My temples ached and I couldn't stop sobbing.

"So does he like me? Yes or no?" was all I managed to ask between one sob and the next.

"Of course! You're so beautiful!"

"I'm beautiful to you. But to him?"

"Well, how could he not like you, can you tell me that?"

"What about Ma? Who's going to tell Ma?" I shouted. I was angry and terribly unsettled.

"One thing at a time." He held out his arms, eyes bulging at my behavior.

"Can I go to bed now?"

"At least tell me whether you want to marry him."

"I'll agree to marrying Erich," I said as I rose from the stool.

"But if you want to marry him, why are you still whining?" he shouted, emptying his pipe.

I couldn't utter another word, so he came over to me and hugged me harder than when I came back from my baccalaureate exams.

"I'm happy, Trina. He's an orphan, poor thing, with the smallest plot of land in the village. In other words, he's all set up to make you go hungry!" He laughed in the hope that at last I'd laugh too.

It took me about a week to recover from that day. When I finally calmed down and things sank in a bit more, I went to Ma and asked, "So can I marry him?"

Ma kept on dusting, and she replied without even turning, "Do what you want, Trina. You've got too much lip for me to even begin to discuss it with you. If you'd wanted my opinion, you'd have asked me before now."

It was as much as I could expect from her.

7

The day Pa walked me to the altar, in the church bedecked with geraniums that Maja had hung everywhere, it was hard for me to hold back my tears. Not because I was emotional, but because on that very day they put Barbara in a car and sent her into exile. They treated her worse than a whore, forcing her to march through the streets in handcuffs. I had on a white dress, starched and covered in frou-frous, my hair was plaited and my shoes shining, while she was disheveled and wore old slippers. The people waiting for me in church thought – all of them, including the priest – that I was running late because I was primping. But I was in the churchyard, crying and begging Pa to take me to Barbara just as I was, so I could tell the *carabinieri* that it was all my fault, and that I should be going into exile too.

"Stop it, child," he repeated patiently, offering me his handkerchief. And if Peppi had not come out at one point to help him drag me bodily to the altar, I might actually have canceled the ceremony.

I went to live in Erich's farmstead, which had belonged to his parents. You could see that it was a house of the dead.

The living room was dark and on the furniture there were photographs of his mother, for ever keeping her eye on me. His mother as a girl, his mother with her children, his mother with her mother. It gave me something to do, changing the look of those rooms. I painted the walls myself and got busy moving the furniture around. Every now and then when I was dragging a piece of furniture, a frame would fall, shattering the glass. I'd sweep up the splinters, kiss the photo of the dead woman in apology and shove it in the bottom drawer, breathing a sigh of relief. In the span of a month I'd put them all away.

There was no lack of space in that farmhouse and outside was a fine field where Grau loved to run. But because it was near the stables, the odor of hay and silage lingered and seeped into your skin; some evenings it made me feel like vomiting. To say nothing of the cold, which in winter made us move like ghosts, our blankets over our shoulders, while the wind gusted under the door with a terrible noise. We were always huddled around the majolica stove, and we washed when we washed. After supper we crawled into bed immediately and almost every night Erich, like a tame animal, drew close to make love. For me it was a ritual and I couldn't say whether I liked it or not. It satisfied him and that was good enough for me. When he made love to me, I sometimes thought of Barbara. I wondered where she'd ended up, and how much she hated me.

I'd get up with him while it was still night and prepare his milk soup, and if he needed it I'd give him a hand milking the beasts and putting out the hay. Getting up early wasn't a problem for me. When I was by myself I'd make another cup of barley coffee and then go to the children. The priest had assigned me to a toolshed behind the butcher's. There were only three students left now. The fascists had carried out new searches across the valley, fined and arrested other teachers. Only the priests – with the excuse of teaching the catechism – could still teach German.

After school I went to my parents' to eat. I often stayed with them; if not, I went back home and read. But Ma couldn't stand me wasting time like that. If she saw me holding a book, she'd grumble that I'd be taking books to hell with me, and she'd saddle me with jobs, nagging me about learning to sew so I'd be ready when children arrived.

On Sundays Erich and I rode our bikes. At the riverbank, we'd fill baskets with mushrooms, clamber up paths to the summits. If I know the valley it's because he led me all over it, not because I was born there. When I felt cold up on the mountaintop, he'd rub my back. He had long, nervous hands and I liked feeling them on me. On holidays, too, he'd wake up at dawn and say, "C'mon, let's go for a walk while the sky is clear." I liked lounging in bed but Erich would prepare the barley coffee, bring it to me in bed and then throw off the sheets.

He told me not to think too much about kids, and when I said that actually I'd like some, he shrugged.

"They'll come when they want to." He cut me short.

No sooner had we had that exchange than I was pregnant. I had just come out of the toolshed when I felt really nauseated, as if I'd got cramp. I quickly pedaled home, ran to the basin – and then indecision got the better of me. I told myself it was better to stay outside, with the result that I vomited at the door.

"I told you they come when *they* decide!" Erich laughed, resting his head on my chest.

I was constantly sleepy while I was pregnant. As soon as I came home from the toolshed, I'd eat something and go to bed. Fear of fascists? It was gone, and even though I was pregnant I certainly didn't want to stop my secret teaching. My tummy made me feel protected, not scared.

When Erich came home from the fields he'd put his hand on my tummy, say that he knew it was a girl and he wanted to call her Anna, like his mother.

"If it's a girl we'll call her Marica," I told him, closing the discussion.

8

At first, Michael ate and slept contentedly in the cradle Pa had made and Ma had filled with cotton padding. He never cried and indeed, he didn't even open his mouth. He uttered his first words when he was three years old. The complete opposite of you. Erich was only good for sweet-talk and getting him to sleep on his shoulder; he wasn't interested in the rest of it. When I asked him why he didn't make the effort to spend a little more time with Michael, he said he wouldn't know what to say to him until he started talking.

It wasn't too much effort for me. I still managed to teach and to walk around with Maja. It was because I could count on Ma, who came to help every morning. But I didn't like her helping me. As soon as she entered the house she'd squeeze my breasts and chide me for being thin. "It stops you producing enough milk," she'd say. And then she was always wanting to hold the baby. No matter what time it was, for her it was always time to feed him.

I had to wait another four years before you were born. For all that time, you were my obsession, and I wanted you even though Ma made me feel like I wasn't a good mother. The day I discovered I was expecting you was the happiest of my life.

I sensed that you were a girl and I was sure I would call you the name I'd read in a novel and which, according to Ma, was another of the whims I'd acquired when I was training to be a teacher.

You were born on a winter's night. The snow was high and the midwife arrived late, when your head was already out. Ma did everything from swapping the buckets to keeping the furnace going so there'd be constant hot water, changing my dressings, giving me time to push and slowing down so as not to tear everything out of me. Even, she then gave orders like a general. But she was thorough and very attentive. She never let go of my hand.

When you were born, the room was filled with the odour of birth and I won't say what else, but I was embarrassed. Ma washed you, cleaned you and put you, a little cap on your head, on my breast. With sweat on her brow and her hands on her hips, she said, "She's exactly like you. You'll have to watch out, and keep her away from the books!" And she laughed, pleased that you weren't red and wrinkly but had doughy white skin.

Erich had been away for days fetching firewood. He'd taken the sled and gone with a group of farmers. I was always nervous when he went to fetch wood. It was dangerous work and more than once, a sled had gone too fast and crashed into a tree or ended up in a gorge. When he came back I told him that Pa had already registered your birth in the town hall and there was no way to change your name now.

"You couldn't have a more headstrong mother," he said, taking you in his arms and studying your face.

You weren't like Michael; you would spit out your milk, and giving you the breast was a struggle every day. I had to squeeze it into your mouth because you got tired of sucking. To get you to sleep we had to rock you constantly and give you a pompom to hold, which Ma tied to your wrist with yarn. According to her, you were afraid of falling and we had to watch you and not leave you alone with your fears. Michael would stand looking at you each evening until you went to sleep. You'd stare at the kerosene lamp, your hazel eyes wide, and then you'd suddenly close them. If you waved your hands in the air he would rub your stomach so you wouldn't wake up. You were in a hurry to speak. Maybe that's why I've always imagined you must be talkative, able to converse with anyone.

At three, you were already haring around. You had endless energy in your legs, so much so that Pa was soon unable to keep up with you. He started to go out and about with Erich, who'd grab you by the collar if you tried to run off. It's one of my clearest memories, watching you walk to church between those two.

I quickly got tired of looking after you and your brother. The lack of time upset me. While I was with you, I told myself, the most wonderful things in the world were happening, and when you were grown I wouldn't be able to go back and rediscover them. Erich didn't understand when I confided such thoughts to him, and said I was making myself bitter.

He never got upset if his supper wasn't ready or the house was messy when he came back from the fields. After he got into his pyjamas he'd take you in his arms and with one hand he'd slice the polenta or fry a couple of eggs in butter. He'd eat standing up. He wasn't bothered about sitting at the table.

He became increasingly fond of you as you grew. You were his trophy. He'd put you on his shoulders and if you weren't yelling in his ear, he'd light a cigarette and go to the piazza like a victorious general. He took Michael with him fishing, or to Karl's inn. He'd let him drink milk from a beer mug so he could feel big.

In the evening, you and your brother would go to the door to wait for him, and when you saw him coming you ran to him and wouldn't even let him come in. He'd dodge you because he still had the stink of animals on him, but you'd put your heads between his legs to show him it didn't matter. You wanted to run around outside with him. I must have seemed boring to you. I liked to put you on the rug and sit there looking at you.

When you were sleepy, you wanted me, and you fell asleep instantly – you on this shoulder, Michael in his cot. Then Erich started smoking and while he smoked he talked in a somber tone. He was obsessed with the fascists.

"They'll send us to work in Africa or fight in some god-forsaken place in their ridiculous empire," he protested, the smoke in his throat. "Right now they're taking our work and our language, but once they've driven us mad and ground us down, they'll boot us out of here and build their wretched dam."

I sat listening to him, not knowing what to say. I could never console him.

"Then we'll take our children and get out of here."

"No!" he growled.

"Why do you want to stay here if we have no work, if we can't speak German, and they destroy our village?"

"Because I was born here, Trina. My father and mother were born here, you were born here, my children were born here. If we leave, they'll have won."

9

In 1936 Erich's sister came to Curon. She had been living in Innsbruck with her husband, a big, tall man with a long mustache. Rich people, city people, whom I'd seen only on our wedding day. Anita and Lorenz were a lot older than we were. They bought one of the many empty farms in the village from the banker. We quickly became close. We ate together on Sundays, sometimes evenings during the week. Anita liked to cook, and would often knock on the door and leave me a ring-shaped cake.

"For the children," she'd say.

She looked like Erich, with his features, the same wide forehead. A small, placid woman who was always smiling. When Lorenz returned from Austria – he was a rep for an insurance company – he'd bring you presents. You couldn't believe your eyes at the sight of some of those toys. You'd say, "Thank you, Uncle Lorenz," hundreds of times, but you didn't feel like hugging him, no doubt because he was so imposing and whiskery. Erich felt at ease with them. He often asked his sister, "What are you planning to do here in Curon?" with the smile of someone who doesn't understand.

"The city was making me confused," Anita told him, studying her hands.

I found Lorenz intimidating. He always wore a brown waistcoat and even when he stayed at home, he put on a bow tie. On nice days he'd invite us to eat out. I'd invent excuses, saying I had to tidy up, but he'd insist and in the end I'd dress you up and we'd go out with them. He talked politics with Erich and I found their discussions difficult to follow. All I understood was that as far as Lorenz was concerned, Germany would save the world. Anita and I walked a few steps behind them. She always talked to me about the two of you, studied your characters and asked me what I had in mind for your futures. I never knew how to answer her. She said your skin was as smooth as porcelain. I too asked her: "Why did you come to Curon?" And then she'd tell me how she'd followed her husband all over Europe for many years and she didn't want to do that anymore. When she confided in me, a sort of melancholy would fall over her and she'd be quiet for a few minutes. Or she'd say, "Always living in different places, I've never made friends with anyone—" and she winced at the thought. I never had the courage to ask her why they didn't have any children.

Michael was a little bull who grew before our eyes. By the age of eleven he was Erich's shadow. He didn't want to go to school anymore and very often he ran off into the fields instead of going to class. If I shouted at him, Lorenz would intervene and say that Michael was doing the right thing.

"The Italian school is worthless. All they do is teach them to praise the Duce. Much better to learn how to work the land," he grumbled in his deep voice.

I had to bite my tongue so as not to say something I'd regret. The thought that Michael wasn't going to school kept me awake at night. It seemed he was living like an animal. Erich, however, didn't worry about it. He took Michael with him, explained how to plant potatoes, how to sow barley and rye, shear sheep and milk cows. Or Pa would take him – he could hardly wait to teach someone his trade.

But you went to school willingly, and you spoke Italian well. In the evenings you rode piggyback on Erich. You'd play, put your hands over his eyes and read his thoughts, which he asked you to interpret. Erich would clap his knobbly hands and throw you up in the air, filling the room with delighted screams. Once when you came home with good marks, you waved your notebook under my nose and said, "Mamma, when I'm big I'm going to be a teacher too. Would you like that?"

Not long ago I found an old photo, a sepia print carelessly stuck to a sheet of paper that must have been in someone's diary. It's a fuzzy photo, and I think Lorenz must have taken it. Michael's in it, hugging me impetuously. But you were hugging Erich.

★

Pa told me that he didn't feel like going to his workshop anymore. His heart couldn't take it, riding his bike to Resia every morning. So I started going instead. I was still out of work, and no longer teaching secretly in the toolshed.

I'd cycle to his carpentry shop and do the administration. I learned to write to the suppliers, pay the workers and keep the ledgers. When there was no one at home, you would go to Aunt Anita's. With you, too, she was placid and smiling. When I came to get you, you would tell me you'd eaten something we couldn't afford: chocolate, prosciutto. There was less and less money in the house, and some evenings we had very little to put on the table. And when we were just married, we counted on my teacher's salary, thinking that one way or another, I'd find a way to teach despite fascism. Then in '38 the animals got sick and we had to kill half of them to prevent contagion. We hardly had any sheep left.

Lorenz wanted to lend us some money but we were too proud to accept it. Erich got it into his head to go to Merano in search of work. Bolzano and Merano really had become what the Duce had in mind. The industrial zones and the suburbs were continually expanding. Lancia, the steelworks and the magnesium industry all moved there. Italians were arriving in their thousands.

"So where do you want to go? Mussolini won't allow anyone to hire Tyroleans," Lorenz kept saying. "It's pointless for you to go all that way."

"The work's there, and they can't refuse to give it to you."

"In fact, they can," Lorenz sighed, scratching his mustache.

Erich punched the wall, shouting that the fascists were bleeding him dry.

"Hitler has already annexed Austria. Let's give him a little more time and he'll come to liberate us too," Lorenz said to reassure him.

10

It seemed like fascism had always existed. There had always been a town hall and a *podestà* with his minions, the walls had always been plastered with the Duce's face, the *carabinieri* had always been nosing into our business and making us go to the piazza for announcements. We were getting used to not being ourselves anymore. Our anger was growing, but as the days flew by it was weakened and diminished by the need to survive. Our anger was turning into melancholy; it never blew up. Placing one's hope in Adolf Hitler was the nearest thing to rebellion. That rebellion made itself felt at the tables in the inn, in the secret hangouts where the men arranged to read German newspapers, but evaporated when they were alone in the stables milking the cows, or when they set off toward the fountain to let them drink.

We coasted along, stifled and apathetic, until the summer of '39, when Hitler's Germans invited us to join the Reich if we wanted, and leave Italy. They called it "the Great Option."

The village celebrated immediately. People rejoiced in the streets, children danced around in rings without knowing why, youths hugged each other, ready to depart, and the men insulted the *carabinieri* in German as they went by. The *carabinieri* kept silent now, hands on their truncheons, heads down. That's how Mussolini wanted it.

Erich spent the day at home, smoking in silence. When Lorenz knocked at the door to say that he was off to the inn to celebrate, Erich didn't go with him. Lorenz came back very late, drunk, and before going home he wanted to speak to Erich. Erich had been asleep for some time and I was in my nightgown, so when I heard him knock I threw a blanket over my shoulders before opening the door. He elbowed me out of the way without a glance and went to our room, leaning against the walls for support. He sat down next to Erich and told him, "Sooner or later I'm going to leave, because I have no roots anywhere. But if this place means something to you, if its streets and mountains belong to you, you shouldn't be afraid to stay." And he embraced Erich's head.

The village was in uproar until the end of the year. No one spoke of anything but leaving, imagining where the Führer might send them and what he would give them in compensation. Which farmsteads, what region of the Reich, how many head of cattle, how much land. They must have been driven mad by the fascists to believe such fibs. The few who, like us, decided to stay were insulted. They called us spies, traitors. All of a sudden, people I'd known from the time I was a little girl stopped greeting me or spat on the ground as I went by. The women who used to go to the river together were now divided into two groups: those who were going for the Option to leave, and the Remainers, and they washed their clothes at different places on the riverbank. Talk about war made tempers flare. After being marginalized and subjugated, we too might become rulers of the world.

I asked Maja, "Are you leaving?"

"I want to leave Curon, but not this way."

"I don't understand what's right anymore," I confided.

"Barbara's family are going," she said, looking away. "To Germany."

How strange it was to hear Barbara's name. It seemed like a century had gone by since we were friends studying Italian by the lake, laughing together on the grass. I had got used to not hearing her name. It was my secret sorrow, something I didn't admit to anyone, not even myself.

They set up booths on opposite sides of the piazza: Nazis next to the belltower, Italians next to the cobbler's shop. Each group distributed leaflets to everyone who approached. The Nazis said to watch out: the Italians would send us to Sicily or to Africa to die like flies. Same thing with the Italians: "The Germans will send you to Galicia, to the Sudetenland or even further east. You'll end up fighting on ice," they said.

Some threw rocks at our windows, which we kept closed now, even during the day. When I think of those years, I remember how dark it was in the house, and how I used to peek through the shutters.

One morning some boys grabbed Michael and beat him

up because he was the son of a Remainer. I found him on the ground in the farmyard, his mouth full of blood, his clothes and his hair covered in mud. The next day I kept you home from school. I took you to the shop on my bicycle and didn't let you out of my sight for an instant.

"I'll teach you myself," I reassured you.

You were upset about it. You told me I was possessive and that no one in your class would hit you because you knew how to get respect. In the shop you kept asking, "Why don't we leave too?"

"Because this is what your father has decided."

"Mamma, I want to leave this place. I can't even go to school here anymore."

11

By the end of the year, some of the villagers had packed their suitcases to go to Germany, rolled and loaded onto carts their lumpy mattresses, dismantled furniture, jute sacks full of dishes and other belongings. In the evenings, men came out of the houses with bags full of clothes carefully folded by the women, who had to cook everything they had for a last hearty meal before leaving. You could smell meat and potatoes, polenta frying in lard. Through their windows you saw families eating without speaking, oil lamps on the table. Those of us who were staying watched them from doorsteps or walking past their fields and realized that even the meat they were eating was poisoning them. They claimed they were happy, that Hitler would make them rich by giving them farms, land and animals. To cheer themselves up, they kept repeating that the Duce would soon build the dam here in Curon, and they'd have to leave anyway. But their stiff upper lips and clenched fists showed how cruel it was to go like this. Cruel for the girls, the children, and even more for the elderly, for whom they reserved the best place on the cart, telling them to get some sleep. When a cart left for the station in Bolzano, or in Innsbruck where the Führer's trains were waiting, the silence of the death knell fell over Curon's streets.

Every evening Gerhard, the village drunk, made a circuit of all the farmhouses – there were around a hundred here in Curon – to see if anyone else had gone. When he found an empty one he'd knock on the door until his knuckles were sore or he fell asleep. Karl would go and wake him up next morning and drag him, completely hammered, to the inn, where he gave him a cup of coffee.

One afternoon Maja said, "Get on your bike. I want to go and say goodbye to Barbara's sister."

When Alexandra saw me at the door with Maja, her eyes opened wide. She invited us in, and cut a slice of bread for each of us. She offered it without giving us a plate or a napkin, like you do with family. We ate the bread in such silence that we could hear the cumin seeds breaking under our teeth. We said goodbye to her mother but she didn't answer. I petted the dog, who was whining near the table.

"Are you going?" Maja asked.

"Yes, but I don't know where yet."

"Have you heard any news about Barbara?" I asked, my eyes downcast.

"She's asked the Duce to pardon her and they're going to let her go soon. She's going directly to Germany without stopping here."

All of a sudden I asked, "Do you have paper and pen?"

"What do you need that for?" Her tone was hostile.

"I want to write her a note."

Alexandra looked at me suspiciously before rummaging through a drawer. She took out a small pad of paper and carefully tore off a sheet. As I wrote, standing and leaning over the table, I felt their eyes on me but it didn't matter.

"Give it to her when you see her," I told Alexandra, folding the sheet in four.

She told me to leave it on the table.

"Give it to her," I repeated, putting it in her hand. "It's very important."

We stood looking at each other for a while. No one spoke. Soon enough, the silence became unbearable. We swallowed the last piece of bread and left.

When I described the scene to Pa, he said, "Child, we're doing the right thing to stay. It doesn't matter if we don't have much to put on the table. Things will get better. The houses we live in belong to us, and we don't have to leave for any reason."

"Are you sure, Pa? They burned down a Remainer's stable, they beat Michael up, and they're waiting for me to send Marica to school so they can do exactly the same to her. Lots of the villagers won't speak to Erich."

"I know, Trina, but it's only temporary. Fascism will pass, those people will leave and we'll go back to living our lives."

It was reassuring to speak with Pa. I wanted Erich to talk to him too, instead of shutting himself up in the house like an outcast. When I went back to the farm that day, I found him pacing nervously as usual.

"The engineers and workers have returned," he said, without even a hello. "All night, the men and lorries kept coming. They've surveyed the length and breadth of Curon, taken soil samples and outlined the perimeter of the dam. Soon they'll start building it. I don't know if anyone in the village has noticed, or if they simply don't care about it because they've decided to leave."

12

That evening I'd come home later than usual. It was already dark outside and the moonlight was reflected in the snow on either side of the road. Our shop had a consignment of furniture for a trattoria, and the workers had labored over it for months. The owner had come with his children and by the time they'd loaded the goods night had fallen. I didn't have a scarf or shawl because it had been bright and sunny that morning, and on my bicycle I felt the cold. I went by Pa's to tell him that everything had gone well. I found him wheezing as he dozed. I patted his shoulder. He smiled at me with his old teeth and told me that Michael had come by and they'd played cards. I was in a hurry to get back, but Pa wouldn't stop asking me questions about how everything had gone, if I'd taken the money, who had come to get the furniture, how Theo and Gustav had worked. Ma put some spätzle under my nose and because I was cold I stayed to eat it. In any case, Erich always bit into the first thing he found as soon as he got home. We rarely ate supper together.

"Your little girl is with your sister-in-law?" Ma asked me without interrupting her knitting. Christmas was coming, and she was making new jumpers as she did every year.

"Today, yes."

"Then take your time eating."

It's true that it was late, but not that late. It must have been about eight-thirty, maybe nine. All the stars were out. Tomorrow, too, would be a sunny day and, distracted as always, I would leave the house without my shawl and then be cold when I went back home. Ma lent me hers, putting it over my shoulders, wishing me a hurried good night and closing the door.

I pedaled all the way to Anita's farm. The light was on.

"Michael is with Erich. Marica fell asleep here," she said, yawning. "We tried to wake her up but she wasn't having it."

She didn't ask me in. Everything happened on the doorstep, under the twinkling stars.

"Did she eat anything?" I asked.

"Yes, polenta in milk. She really wanted that—" and she smiled her usual smile, full of a peace I couldn't find. I was happy when you ate milk and polenta; for me it was proof that you didn't look down on what we had.

In the distance we saw someone bustling about, loading a cart. One more farm left empty.

At home, Erich and Michael were asleep. I climbed into bed, thinking that maybe I'd made a mistake, and that the next day we could have breakfast together, take our time getting up. On Sunday Erich made hot milk for us, and it was one of the nicest moments of the week. Michael always acted the clown, talking with his mouth full, and you amused yourself by dunking your polenta in his bowl.

"Marica stayed there?" Erich asked.

"Yes – Anita said you'd wanted to wake her but she was too sleepy."

He turned over and a moment later, he was snoring again. I didn't sleep a wink, whether because you were with Anita and Lorenz or because I lived in fear of the Leavers burning down the stables and killing our animals. I heard the village wake up slowly, the first strike of the bell. I saw the sun come up over the mountains. I turned over in bed. I was thinking, today I'll put the milk on myself, and I tried to invent a reason for going to get you. If I waited for you, I'd have to wait till lunchtime. You liked being with your aunt and uncle; they made a fuss of you, showered you with gifts. Everything we couldn't give you ourselves.

When it was light, Erich woke up and started talking to me softly. Outside the snow was high. And when I asked him, "Will you go and get Marica?" he told me to let you sleep a bit more. He made breakfast, and the three of us ate it together. Maybe I waited because it was so rare for us to be alone with Michael, and in his way he needed our attention and wanted to enjoy the moment. At nine I got dressed, put on that brown skirt you liked, put up my hair any old way and went out. I left those two at the table eating more polenta.

There, in front of their house, I understood immediately. The doors were just drawn to. The windows closed but not bolted. On the ground, an upturned hat full of snowflakes. I saw before me all the dark and emptiness that must have been gathering in that house, which I hadn't even been brave enough to enter. I ran to Erich and dragged him there to see. Michael came too, and called out your name in the deserted rooms. I clenched my fists and tried to cry, but the tears wouldn't come. I punched the walls so hard I hurt myself. Scratched until I split my nails. Until Erich pulled me away.

People from the other farms came round. I kept saying Michael's name, wanting him near me for fear that they'd take him too. They laid me out on the bed, took off my muddy shoes. I covered my face with my hands to block the white light coming into the room. I came to with Ma sitting beside the bed as if I were dying. Erich kept telling me to calm down.

Evening fell, then night. Those who said that you were still somewhere nearby fell silent. Those who said that you would come back stopped saying so. About ten men left to look for you. Erich rode his bike all the way to Malles and reported what had happened at the fascists' headquarters. When he got back the next day, his face looked like death, and he seemed all alone against the world.

I sat staring into space. My throat was parched and I held back a cough. I shut my eyes in order not to hear the words that hit me like words I'd already heard: "According to the logbooks, they decided to go to the Reich. Their train has already left."

Part Two

The Escape

1

I won't describe your absence. I won't say a single word about the years we spent looking for you, the days we stood at the doorway, staring down the road. I won't tell you about your father, who leaves the house without saying goodbye to me. They stop him at the station in Bolzano as he tries to board a goods train bound for Berlin. The Italian police first throw him in jail, then promise they'll bring her back to him, his Marica. A few days later he tries to cross the border on foot. The torches blind him, but he doesn't stop at "Halt!" He's grazed by a bullet. Afternoon, and soldiers knock at the door, wrapped in mouse-gray coats, their ranks sewn on their chests. Before shoving him into the farmhouse they threaten to intern him in the asylum in Pergine, the same one that Hitler will later clear of inmates, deporting them to the camps and gassing them. I won't talk about Michael, who carries your photo everywhere with him – one without a border from the previous year, showing your hair pulled back in a style you didn't wear anymore – and spends his days with a gang of brats, showing it to everyone in the neighboring villages. I won't tell you about the months when one of us would abruptly run off without telling the others and then think, on finding the house empty, that sooner or later the woods would swallow us up. Lost for ever in the senseless attempt to bring you back here. Where you no longer wanted to live.

One morning the postman runs to hand me a letter. On the envelope, only my name – no stamp, no franking. The writing I know: it's yours.

"Someone left it at the door of the post office," he says, without looking at me.

"Who?" I ask him, snatching it out of his hand.

"I don't know."

I try to keep my hands from shaking. For some reason I think of Ma opening my letters with a hot iron to see whether they were from a girlfriend or a man.

Dear Mamma,

I'm alone in my room as I write. I was the one who wanted to leave with Aunt Anita and Uncle Lorenz. We knew you wouldn't give your permission, which is why we fled. Here in the city, I'll be able to study and improve myself. Don't feel bad for me, because I'm fine and one day I'll come back to Curon. If the war lasts a long time, don't worry: I'm safe here. When I knock on your door, I hope that you, Papa and Michael will still love me. Aunt and

Uncle make sure I have everything I need. Forgive them if you can. And forgive me, too.

Marica

From that day on, my pain changes. Michael rips up your picture and asks us not to talk to him about you anymore. Not even to mention you. Erich stops running back and forth, doesn't try to leave the country, no longer tries to find you. He sits at the window smoking, doesn't even go out to feed the animals. He opens the shutters in the morning and closes them at night. Between those two actions nothing else happens. I stay in bed, shutters partially open, door locked. I feel like I have no more tears. I read your letter over and over, keeping it with me. I relive that night, unable to make peace with it. I wonder how I could have failed to hear your voice, the footsteps of those bastards, the sound of bags being loaded onto a cart, the horses snorting while they wait or the rumble of an automobile starting up. How is it possible that no one in Curon heard you? Were you awake, or did they put you on the cart asleep? Did you want to leave or did they force you? Did you write that letter yourself, or did they make you write it?

Pa knocks at the door one day and tells me to go out and buy him a pinch of tobacco. He sits down beside Erich, says nothing. They sit still like that at the window, watching the clouds. Then Pa takes Erich's arm and walks him to the stables to feed the animals, to caress them, one by one. Before going home he rejoins me, asks me to get some supper and lay the table. Next to the kitchen sink he leaves a basket with some meat in it, a loaf of bread, some wine.

The pain makes me feel dizzy. Something familiar and secret all at once, something we never talk about. Over the years, whenever we happen to forget the words of that letter, we will try again to find you, knowing, now, that this lonely search is only obedience to a hope we no longer feel.

No, you don't deserve to know about those dark days. You don't deserve to know how we cried out your name. How many times we clung to the illusion that we were on the right path. There's no reason to relive this story in words. I'll tell you instead about our lives, about how we survived. I'll talk to you about what happened here in Curon. In the village that no longer exists.

2

War broke out. Many of those who'd decided to leave for Germany ended up staying here. Fear of the unknown, the lies told as propaganda and Hitler's rage kept them in Curon.

A brief, dull light illuminated the January days. They all began with long, grey dawns. You could see the snowy peak on Ortler and lower down, the tips of the trees bent under the icy wind. People in the village didn't seem worried, just more exhausted. Tired of the fascists, tired of stumbling around in the dark.

I sewed with Ma, who never left my side. She taught me to knit and we'd sit together for many hours in silence, elbow to elbow on the kitchen chairs I always forgot to stuff with straw. She didn't want me to talk about you. When there wasn't any sewing to do, she'd put a basket on my head and take me to the river to wash the banker's clothes. If I got lost looking into the distance, she'd insist that I wring the clothes harder, until my bad thoughts vanished.

"God made us with our eyes in front for a reason! That's the direction we need to look in. Otherwise he'd have put them on the side, like fish!" she would say severely.

She'd started working in the fields at nine years old, and

had spent her evenings nailing up fruit boxes. To her, you were selfish: you'd chosen those with the most money.

An accomplice.

Everyone thought things would go as they had in 1915: while the Italians and Austrians were killing each other on the Karst, here in Curon we continued to gather hay, cut grass and put it out to dry on the walls, take the cows up to the mountain huts, fill buckets with milk and make butter from it, slaughter pigs and eat sausages and salami for days on end. The children of the poor continued to cross the border, working as shepherds in exchange for a pair of shoes, a fistful of coins, some clothes. Their mothers waited for them, counting the days until the feast day of San Martino in November, when everyone came back home and the village celebrated until evening. We waited for summer to melt the snow and then for the Alpine wind to bring it back, still and heavy. We buried our dead in silence. We swallowed the bitter pill of having fought for the Austrians only to find ourselves Italian. We put up with all this because we were convinced it was the last war, the war to end all wars. So news of a second conflict with Germany, which was soon to take over the world, left us momentarily stunned. But we deluded ourselves that the mountains would yet again wall us off, and that this Italy we were meant to belong to would stay neutral until the end. And at first, news of the war brought a certain relief to the village: "At least now they'll stop going on about the dam," "Now they'll have something else to think about," "Our animals and farms will finally be safe." That's what the men said at the inn. And the women in front of the church. Some in Curon even celebrated the start of the war. Gerhard walked around with his flask, waving it high and crying, "War for them, peace for us!"

Now that Hitler's armies were on the move, the people who'd stayed felt smug about their choice, imagining that those who'd emigrated to Germany would be fighting on the eastern front or sinking into the mud somewhere in Europe.

And when the war broke out, the Italians finally stopped coming here. Of course the *carabinieri*'s trucks were always around, a frenetic toing and froing of military vehicles, foreshadowing what we most feared, but those arrogant people carrying their suitcases had disappeared.

We spent our first Christmas without you at Ma and Pa's. They'd made gnocchi and chicken broth. We ate in silence, and there was never such silence at a holiday meal. Pa quickly got rid of the friends and clients who came by with good wishes. We'd heard the pipers going through the villages in the valley, the music you and your brother had danced to in the street the year before with the other children. Ma cooked, sewed, went back and forth to the river, never stopping for a second. I don't know where she found all her energy. All of a sudden she didn't seem old to me anymore. Every now and then, when we were alone, I'd break down crying and she'd take my hand. I'd never felt so much the daughter as after you ran away.

*

That winter, too, passed. In April the sun looked like a crystal lamp, and the chimney sweep went from farm to farm fixing the guttering. We didn't light our fire now because the village envied us. The others used twigs and brushwood, and we had the wood from trees that Michael brought back from Pa's workshop. He'd learned the trade and left school. The workers said he was a skilled carpenter for someone of fifteen.

The ice-encrusted fields turned green again but it was harder than ever to work with the animals. The milk remained in the buckets for days and we could no longer sell it, not even a liter. Erich kicked angrily at the buckets and I kept silent, watching the mud suck up the white stains squelching under the cows' hooves.

I continued to unsnarl the wool and pile it up on the ground. An old man with watery eyes and rounded shoulders would come to collect it. He paid us a pittance, but at least we were able to keep warm. With that wool he made uniforms and kit for the soldiers.

"There will be more work when Italy enters the war," he said, loading the wool on his three-wheeled van.

"And when will Italy enter the war?" Ma asked fervently, as if it were the old man's decision.

His crooked face twisted in a grimace, and he went off again on his three-wheeler, leaving behind a musty smell that hung on the air.

Anyway, aside from what the old man said, there were

so many roadblocks that we too felt, day by day, hour after hour, that war was threatening. In the evenings, the airplanes beyond the mountains sounded like swarms of hornets and Ma said we should take shelter in the stables, where she had filled a trunk with straw and blankets.

"The bombs might fall on Curon by mistake since it's so close to Austria!" she said in a panic.

"Go to the stables yourself. I want to die in my bed, not surrounded by the smell of shit!" Pa would shout, his voice growing increasingly hoarse.

One morning I waited for Ma and she didn't come. At lunchtime I went to the farm. The door was open but there was nobody by the stove. I called her but she didn't come and she didn't answer. I called again, my eyes fixed on the copper pots hanging on the walls. When I finally decided to go to her room, I found her on the bed, curled up next to Pa, who was already dressed in his blue suit, the one he'd worn to my wedding. She'd shaved him and combed his hair. She was crying softly against his shoulder, and when she started crying harder she took his head in her hands as if it were a sparrow's.

"He died in his sleep."

"Why didn't you come and get me?"

"He died last night."

"Why didn't you come and get me?" I asked again.

When she finally turned over, she took my hand and put it on Pa's, which was still warm. She held him even closer, and somehow I, too, found myself lying on a corner of the bed. I caught the odor of Ma's clothes, that of ash from the stove. I listened to her crying, and every now and then I felt courageous enough to take Pa's hand again, now getting colder.

At the funeral, Theo and Gustav carried his coffin with Erich and Peppi. Michael was proud of having made it. "Grandpa will sleep the sleep of the just in there," he told me.

3

On a spring morning in 1940 notices went up on the walls of the town hall. Italian words, as usual, as if thumbing the nose at the people who came near to read them. A few stopped to glance at the posters, muttered and kicked a stone, then left on their carts piled with hay, or carrying pails of milk. Only a few in Curon knew how to read, and no one understood that language, the language of hate.

Erich marched into the house and quickly pulled me outside. I walked slowly in the blinding sun, but he was pulling me so hard that I fell down a few times. When we stood in front of the noticeboard at the town hall, he ordered me to read out what was written there. It was unpleasant to voice words he didn't want to hear, and I didn't think it was nice of him to get me to translate them. The notice said that it would remain on the wall for eight days before being removed. It said that this was an official announcement and that we must take note of it. And it said that permission to begin construction of the dam had been granted by order of the Italian government.

Erich listened to me, rigid, his eyes narrowed to pinpricks. I stood stock still, watching him study the notice, with all those incomprehensible words.

"Curon and Resia will cease to exist," he observed, swallowing the smoke of his cigarette.

He took me back home. I watched him set off toward the valley, and once more he seemed deathlike and alone against the world. When he came back that evening, he flopped down and didn't even take off his muddy shoes. He drank a lot of water and ate his polenta in milk. I didn't know how to break into his silence, and I waited awkwardly for him to say something. I'd felt the same way when I'd tried unsuccessfully to console him.

"The villagers are confident. They say the project will change. That it's just one of the usual announcements. At the inn, Karl's saying that you don't start building dams with war on the way."

"Maybe he's right," I replied.

"They're all idiots!" he cried. "They'd come up with any reason to avoid lifting a finger!"

"Why do you say that?"

"The fascists and Montecatini know war's threatening, that we men will soon leave to fight, that nobody here understands Italian, and we're just peasants! It's the right moment to take advantage of us."

Three lorries came down the road that led to Merano. They were the color of iron, and their huge wheels raised clouds of dust. They went back and forth to Resia, all day long. The strangers spoke to each other in Italian, spreading their arms and pointing into the distance as if tracking swallows. The men were in the fields, and we women stood at our doors, watching them chatter in their language. Some of us got worked up, as if they were going through our drawers: our village was so small and old it seemed like a house. We looked at each other to pluck up our courage, and then ordered some of our snotty-nosed kids to run to the fields and get the men. The farmers whistled to other farmers. By mid-afternoon, there was no one left hoeing, the stables were full and the animals, cooped up, leaned against each other moaning. Erich was the last to arrive. Arms crossed, he stood listening to a youth trying to ask in Italian what the men had come to do. Meanwhile, the workers were drawing crosses on the ground in whitewash, which stuck to the mud. When they passed us they tried not to hear our voices, which irritated them. The peasants threw each other sidelong glances, becoming increasingly nervous as the hours went by, rubbing their hands and clenching their fists. Our houses, the church, the roads – everything lay between the borders marked out by crosses, and their meaning was unclear to us. Beyond, there was nothing but the foothills and the larches, bent over by the incessant wind.

A few evenings later, two guys wearing jackets and ties got out of a black automobile. One was lean, the other fat. They invited us to the inn and we followed like sheep. As soon as they sat down we circled, forming a crowd around them. In German, they ordered a mug of beer for each of us. We drank, some hesitantly and some all in one go.

"We're here from Rome," they continued in our language. "The government has approved an old order for the construction of a dam."

"It's a complex system of dams that will affect many of the villages in this valley."

They spoke in labored and precise German, a few words at a time, before sipping their beer and wiping the foam from their lips with the backs of their hairy hands. I held on to Erich's arm; he insisted I stay.

"How many meters will the water level rise?" asked a farmer.

"We don't know yet."

"And what if the water covers our houses?" asked another.

"We'll build others nearby," said the lean one.

"Bigger, modern ones," added the fat guy, who had a thin mustache and an air of indifference to his own words. "However, there's no reason for you to be worried now. This sort of work goes on for years, sometimes decades," he added, looking into his mug.

All at once the farmers started speaking over one another. The two men in their fine wool suits smiled at our boorish ways, unperturbed. They waited for the chaos to die down before adding, "Anyone who loses his land will receive compensation."

Someone shouted that their cows didn't eat compensation. Others slammed their fists down, swearing and saying that without the fields, their animals would die of hunger.

"So what if we don't accept your compensation?" Erich asked.

Everyone fell silent. The two men slowly emptied their mugs and shrugged their shoulders. They looked at us blankly. The silence was now so strained that one wrong word would have turned it into a brawl. Once more the men cleaned their mouths with the backs of their hands. At last they stood up and plowed through the crowd.

Some were brave enough to repeat the question only when they were outside the inn, where the scent of wet earth and hay was penetrating. The air relaxed the villagers, the sight of the belltower elicited deep sighs. In the distance you could see the women behind windows fogged with their breath, babies asleep in their arms.

Before getting into the car the lean one said, "If you don't accept the compensation, there'll be problems."

"There's a law called forced expropriation," the fat guy announced, slamming the door.

When the automobile left, the air no longer smelled of wet earth nor of hay; it stank of diesel. We stood there coughing until the automobile disappeared around the bend.

Erich and I walked home in silence. The moon looked like it had been hung against a cascade of stars. Crickets chirruped in chorus.

"The day comes when you have to kill someone in order to preserve your dignity," he said, dropping a match.

4

I did not go to the piazza to hear the *podestà* read out the declaration of our entry into the war. I stayed at home with Ma, making piles of wool. Not many weeks later the baker's son – one of the few who, like us and Maja's family, had decided to stay – found in his letterbox a call-up notice for the front. Fear of receiving the card from the damned Royal Army immediately spread through the village. When an official messenger, a motorcycle or a police jeep went by, some women went out into the streets like sentries, their hands covered with flour and their hair put up hastily. Others instinctively closed their shutters and ran to get into bed. Erich said they'd soon come for him too.

That's why the armored vehicles crossing our valley suddenly started to terrify me. I stood at the door looking at the soldiers packed into lorries, jaws squared under helmets shining in the sun, hands clasping machine guns strapped over their shoulders. Their dark faces were hardened by cropped hair and close shaves, and I thought back to when these were just the anonymous faces of young lads with messy hair and days-old beards who chased after young girls without a thought for war.

Erich was quiet. He smoked like a chimney and sighed softly. He was more worried about leaving us on our own than about going to the front.

"If they enlist me, take care of Michael," he'd say before going to sleep. "Don't think about anything else."

That anything else was you.

Those months went by sluggishly, anxiously. We were all mired in endless waiting. It wore us out and kept us hidden inside our houses. I missed Pa, his good-natured smile, his ability to make me see things from another perspective. Erich wasn't like that. For him everything was hand-to-hand combat, and only those who gave their all – even when defeat had already been decided by fate – could be called courageous.

Michael, meanwhile, was becoming a man, with a low voice and broad shoulders. He started to develop a strange distrust of us. As soon as he came home from work he'd change and go out and about with young men I'd never seen and who didn't live in Curon. Erich told me that they were all Nazis and that they'd enlist as soon as possible; scum, he said, both crueler and more reckless than simple soldiers.

"What have the Nazis ever done to you? Do you prefer the Duce's Blackshirts?" I asked him.

He shook his head, pressing his palms against his temples. "They'll do everyone harm, Trina."

When Michael went out I'd ask him, "At least tell me where you're going."

"Out," he would answer cockily, and he'd look at me in such a way that I didn't have the energy to persist.

The news-sheets arriving in the village in the autumn of '40 spoke of Italo-German victories, but also of the long road ahead to defeat the Allies. The fascist officials went around delivering call-up notices with the names and surnames of recruits. If they found us women they made it clear that not showing up would mean facing the firing squad as a deserter. The soldiers one saw no longer had the faces of young boys with squared jaws, but heavy hands and scowls that made you look away. War had changed them.

They came to our farm one day in October. The sky was clear and the faraway rumble of airplanes sounded like a thunderstorm. There were two of them and while they were asking me questions, they cocked their ears to catch noise from inside.

"We're looking for Erich Hauser."

"He's not here."

"He's to present himself at the barracks in Malles."

The night before he left, Erich wanted to make love, but he did it angrily, without letting himself go. Afterward he stayed up, smoking in the dark room.

"Watch out for Michael," he repeated.

They sent him to Cadore and from there to Albania, and then to Greece, where those asinine fascists couldn't have taken an inch of land if the Germans hadn't come to their rescue. They'd said it was an easy front, yet many died on the battlefield or came home wounded.

From time to time a letter would arrive. Sometimes the censors had struck out everything and all you could read of the entire page was the final line: "Give Michael a hug from me. Your Erich Hauser."

I asked Ma to come and stay with me. She put insoles in Erich's shoes to make them fit me, and in the morning she'd wrap a big scarf around my neck that came down to my feet when it was unwound. I'd let out the cows along with the few sheep we had left, and drag the herd outside. The fields down in the valley were still green, and when I was outside it was hard to believe that there was a war on or that Erich had been conscripted. In the pasture I met flocks led by the old men left at home. Men of Ma's age, who'd had to summon up their strength once more because their sons were at the front and there were no other men to take care of the women and grandchildren.

When I sat on a rock to eat bread and cheese, I felt as if I were Erich, as if I had the same thoughts. Sometimes I stared at the sky long enough to convince myself that I'd always been a farmer. I'd turn to look at the village, small from up there on the hill, and be overtaken by Erich's feelings: this was my land, no one could drive me from it, and I couldn't just stand idly by and watch. I considered the fascists bastards because they wanted to drown us, they'd dragged us into the war and taken Barbara away. The Nazis were just as bad.

They'd pitched us against each other, and they wanted our men but only as cannon fodder.

At dusk, I'd return with the flock and Grau; by now his coat was saggy and he couldn't run like he used to. I'd stop for a moment, and from a distance watch the laborers setting up the construction site for the dam, on the edge of the village, near the river. The war hadn't stopped them. On the contrary, now they were even working in the dark. They set huge floodlights on the ground and from a distance the glare looked like it was coming from a great fire. There were about a hundred laborers and they were living in shacks put up by the Montecatini company. They had no contact with us. They were like moles. They unloaded pipes, sacks of cement, shovels. Meanwhile the lorries came and went, the bulldozers and caterpillars looking like monsters. No cowbells jingled, blades of grass rustled in the valley. The noise of lorries and caterpillar trucks had killed off the silence.

People in Curon didn't speak about the dam anymore. It took half an hour to get to the river by bike, but no one ever cycled that far. As far as the farmers and shepherds were concerned, the laborers didn't exist. The old men denied that there were men down there.

I lost track of how many times Erich had said, "The people hushing it up are letting the horror advance every day."

Since he'd gone, I felt like an alley cat. I, too, stank of sweat and stables, and my hands were calloused. I'd developed rough habits. I never looked at myself in the mirror anymore and I always had on the same torn jumper, my scarf over my nose, hair held up with a wooden stick.

On Saturdays women would knock on my door with letters from their husbands, and I sat at the table to read them out. To tell the truth, there wasn't much to read because the censors struck through almost everything. But they were stubborn, and they'd grab the paper from my hand and put it against the light, saying they could see some marks. So to get them out of my hair I'd make things up. I'd say that their men were doing well, were eating every day and weren't too involved in the fighting. Or that they weren't sure where they were but that the mess was decent and they'd be home soon. I'd close with silly sweet talk so the wives would go home feeling cheery. One of them, Claudia, would open her eyes wide and exclaim, "The front has made him romantic!" and she'd go away bemused. The women would leave coins to thank me and I'd give them to Ma. I wasn't interested in being charitable.

When the house was empty again I'd open the windows to let out the stale air. I'd sit down on the chair and look at the room. When I felt like writing, I no longer wrote to you. Writing to your father seemed to erase you.

5

My brother, Peppi, managed to avoid conscription. When he got the call-up notice, he ate nothing but licorice for days. He showed up for his medical pissing green, and with a fever of 40 degrees. Just a little more and he'd have died of the poison. Peppi ended up as a builder near Sondrio, working for a small company building prefabs for headquarters. He came to see us one rainy day, traveling by coach. With him was a tiny young girl with sky-blue eyes. She was elegant, and her name was Irene, like Ma's. He told us right away that they wanted to get married, something that by that point I didn't believe in anymore. I thought Peppi just wanted to get lost in the world.

There were ten of us at the wedding. Ma asked me to do myself up that day, and she lent me the pearl necklace she'd worn at her wedding. In the trattoria I sat next to Ma because Irene's family spoke a strange dialect and I did my best to give her a rough translation of what little I understood. I ate everything, but only to fill my stomach. I'd become wild and solitary, I worried about the animals and couldn't wait to get back to them. The geraniums in the dining room made me feel melancholy. Maja's face came to mind, and the memory of Barbara's kisses. Erich came to mind too; on our wedding day he'd worn a bow tie so tight that I couldn't wait to take it off him. And I thought of you, at the time a desire I didn't even know I had.

When lunch was over, my brother said he was happy to have married Irene and that he really would have had a terrible life without her. For some reason, the years had flown by, and Peppi and I had never acted like siblings. We had always loved each other, at least in theory. Peppi told me that he often thought about how we'd all spent Sundays together or when he'd tickled Ma's large hips because he was fed up with her not laughing at his pranks. He said that he was happy in Sondrio and didn't miss Curon very much. "I like being a builder. Pa would be pleased with me."

"He was already happy with you. You were his pet."

"Do you remember what a temper he had!?"

"But he was soft as butter!" I protested.

"With you, maybe. With me he was harder than nails!" he exclaimed, laughing to himself.

The next day I went with him to take flowers to the cemetery. On the way he reassured me that Erich would be back soon, safe and sound; we were all safe with Hitler, even the Italian soldiers.

"I poisoned myself with licorice because I'm a coward, but I have faith in Hitler," he said, looking at Pa's tombstone.

"If you had enlisted he'd have sent you to Silesia, or who knows where, like all the others who left for the Reich in '39."

"I'm confident that the war will end well for us," he repeated, as if I hadn't spoken.

"He, on the other hand, didn't have a scrap of that confidence," I replied, pointing to Pa's tomb.

When Peppi, Irene and her family got back on the coach I went to the stables to milk the cows, but my hands were sore. Ma came to help, explaining that if I didn't milk them, the cows would get mastitis. I'd find them lying ill on the ground, and their lowing would wake us up in the middle of the night. So I got busy, frenetically squeezing their udders until I no longer felt the pain in my palms. Ma patted me on the back even as she scolded me. "Be strong, girl. Don't think too much." As far as she was concerned, thoughts were your greatest enemy.

Maja came to see me on Wednesdays. I'd come down from the mountains before the shadows climbed up the side of the Ortler, wash off the sweat and put on a clean dress. Ma was happy when Maja came. She made cream and she'd put a spoonful on our milk.

"Finish it all up because tomorrow it will be hard and I'll have to cut it with a knife," she'd say.

Maja and I would ride our bikes to the river. Keeping an eye on the construction site was a way to feel close to Erich. The caterpillar trucks had torn everything up, felled the larches and the firs, dug an enormous channel. The lorries came and went from Vallelunga loaded with earth and rocks from the quarry, which they tipped into the holes. It was easier now to imagine the dam. In San Valentino they'd built an enormous dam and created a reservoir, which fed the power plants in

Glorenza and Castelbello. Maja and I looked on speechless. We watched the laborers moving around, busy as bees, marking the ground over which the bulldozers drove, raising flurries of dust. If we asked questions, the *carabinieri* on duty would raise an eyebrow but they wouldn't answer. One bright Sunday we went out for the whole day and eventually got as far as Glorenza. There were construction sites there too, cars and hundreds of laborers mechanically executing the same movements. It seemed as if the entire valley had been taken hostage. Under cover of silence, before our very eyes.

When we turned back home I told Maja that the laborers were no doubt extremely poor, and who knew how many of them were destitute, coming up here from the Veneto, the Abruzzo or from Calabria. Building the dam was a bit of luck for them, guaranteed work for months, years, maybe, and avoiding the front. Maja grew thoughtful and her thin lips turned down in a frown.

"It's hard to know who to be angry with around here," she fumed.

We kept going to check on the site until winter returned and the roads became impossible to travel by bicycle. We'd skid on every curve and our wheels spun round and round. We ended up throwing snow at each other, laughing when it went down our clothes. With every snowball we'd yell: "Fuck the war!" "Fuck the fascists!" "Fuck the dam!" and we kept on until our arms ached and our fingers froze.

I was lazy, but Maja wanted to go out even in the winter. She liked walking over the frozen lake. Ma wouldn't give me the time to decide if I wanted to go before she chased me out, like a mouse from the stables.

"Go on, you two, I have to mop the floor and you're in my way!" she'd say.

I went out to make her happy, but as soon as I got outside I'd beg Maja to take me to her farm because I didn't really want to see the frozen lake. One look was enough to make me dream, at night, of walking on it with you. It was a lovely dream, but I was afraid of repeating it. You and I are crossing it hand in hand until we step on a crack. We fall through, but we don't die. We're left swimming in the tepid water. Weightlessly. Once more, we're the whole world to one another.

At Maja's house we sat in front of a humming stove. She'd throw some branches on the fire and I would feel the blood flow slowly back into my fingertips. When she stoked the fire with the poker, light flecked the walls and lit up her tousled hair. With Maja I could talk about you. I used to tell her what you were like, describing your character and the sharp answers you could come up with for a girl of ten.

"Now I wouldn't recognize her on the street. She must be a woman by now, and she'll already have forgotten her childhood," I said with an odd sense of shame.

Maja would listen without saying a word, sighing, her head tipped back. When I couldn't stand her silence any longer I'd put your letter in her hand and she'd tell me to throw away the damned letter, once and for all. When I asked her to tell me my faults, she'd reply that life is a ragbag of chances and it makes no sense to talk about faults. She'd suddenly stand up, rub my cheeks and ask me to help her make *canederli* or apple compote.

One day, however, she interrupted brusquely, saying that she was fed up of my complaining and couldn't bear it any longer.

"You have to put up with suffering, go right to the bitter end – further than you ever go!" she cried. "You have to end up wanting to throw your life to the dogs, because that's the only way you'll find peace again! Don't you know that having a child means being prepared for the worst kind of suffering? Do I have to explain to you that children are separate beings? Anyway, at least you had kids, but for me that time has passed. No one will come and see me when I'm old. I'll just sit and stare at the fire in the stove like a moron!"

I sat there watching her cry with rage, and I wanted to run home. But when I got up, she stood between me and the door, hanging her head. "I'm sorry, Trina. I didn't mean it. But maybe you shouldn't talk to me about your daughter anymore because I don't know how to console you."

6

At the beginning of '42, I stopped getting letters. Some nights I dreamed I saw Erich coming home with you. You loomed up hand in hand on the road that goes to Switzerland.

I felt I'd always lived like this. Taking the animals to pasture, hoeing in the garden, unraveling the wool – the rest I left for Michael to decide. He was bringing home money and he liked having his say. In reality, he was just another poor devil himself, shut up in a workshop from dawn to dusk, with wood dust getting into his lungs. I found a picture of the Führer in his wallet.

Once a month, the women with husbands or sons at the front got together. To make Ma happy, I'd put on my jacket but I dragged my feet like a bear. We went to someone's home and we did nothing but pray, or else I'd have to stand and read and reread the letters they shoved under my nose, which never really said anything. I left feeling dazed, and I was dying to go back to tend the stables and milk my cows in peace. I began to convince myself that it would be better to imagine Erich dead – that way I could rejoice if he came back. With or without you.

*

The old man who used to come and collect the piles of wool started sending his son. He was a tall, thin kid with shoulder blades that stuck out of his jumper. His eyes were kind and he always called me by my name. He was younger than me and his skin was still a bit spotty with youth. As time went by, he got into the habit of coming into the house, and each time he tried to lengthen the conversation even though he didn't know what to say. One day Ma offered him a hot drink, and in the time it took her to go to the kitchen and boil the water, he put his hand on my knee and told me earnestly that he wanted to take care of me. I sat staring into his sweet eyes.

"What do you mean, take care of me?"

"I'll pay more for your wool. Two, three, even four times more."

I broke out laughing and told him that if he wanted to pay four times more for the wool, I had nothing against it and he could start right in that day. He was upset and his eyes turned dreamy. He sat looking at me, his mouth hanging open, and I didn't know whether to excuse myself or keep laughing at his foolishness. Then all of a sudden he came over to my chair, put his hand on my leg again and said he never knew how to explain himself with women.

"Can I give you a hand unloading the hay?" he asked when Ma took our cups from us.

Unloading the hay and distributing it between the mangers was a job I hated, so I said yes. As soon as we were in there he bolted the door. Near the haystack he held my shoulders and kissed my face all over. He seemed too young and too thin to do me any harm, so I let him kiss me. Even his mouth had a sweet taste, and the smell of someone else's breath, the flesh of someone other than Erich told me that I was yearning to let go. He laid me down on the hay, kissed my neck and squeezed my breasts with hands cracked with the cold. In an instant he was on top of me and while he made love, he told me he loved me and wanted to take care of me. I put my hand over his mouth: I wanted to feel the warmth of his body, his carefree, youthful passion and the tips of hay tangled in my hair and prickling through my jumper, which would hold his scent for days.

"It mustn't happen again," I told him when it was over.

"Not even if your husband doesn't come back from the war?"

"My husband is coming back," I answered, opening the door and shooing him out.

To keep him from coming in again, I would stand in front of the door and wait for him, watching the road with an irritated expression that wasn't like me. When his three-wheeler showed up, I'd motion for him to wait; there was no need for him to get out. Watching me walk hunched under all the wool I'd piled onto a canvas and slung over my shoulder, the old man would chuckle and elbow his son. His crooked smile made me want to stuff his mouth with wool. The youth watched me, troubled. After a few weeks he started loading the heaps of wool, fast and furious, and he'd put the money in my hand with contempt, never meeting my eye. Ma said it was better not to let any man come in, because during wartime they have evil intentions.

"They leave us by ourselves, and then they get upset if certain things happen," she'd say as she went on darning. "They gather like vultures, waiting for you to slip up so they can treat you like a whore for the rest of your life."

I froze when I heard her, uncertain whether she was saying that because she knew what I'd done in the hay or if it was only her fear.

Every now and then Anna, the wife of the blacksmith, would come and see us. She was a tall woman with narrow lips and a pointy chin. Usually she came to learn how to sew, but one morning she showed up holding the hand of a little kid who couldn't have been ten years old.

"He's my youngest son," she said without entering. "Every time the teacher speaks to him, he answers in German and he's got sores on his hands from being beaten with a stick." She pried open his reddened palms, which he kept shut as if he were hiding a stolen coin.

"Teach him a little Italian," she begged me. "At least whatever he needs to escape further beatings. I'm worried that sooner or later my husband will do something he'll regret."

"I can't teach him for free," I told her.

She nodded. "I don't have any money to give you, but I'll bring salami, eggs and whatever I can pick up on my way."

Ma appeared at the door and put some bread with sugar in his hand. He tucked into it on the spot.

"You'll give us what you can. Don't worry." Ma cut things short and asked her in.

I looked at her, shocked. No matter whether I was a child or a woman, Ma would always treat me the same. Assertive and authoritarian. She would always show up behind me to get me out of a tight spot. And not because she liked doing it, but because according to her I couldn't allow myself the luxury of being so indecisive.

"If you wanted to be indecisive you shouldn't have married a farmer!" she'd tease.

I didn't like teaching Italian that much, but sitting at the table for a few hours with that lazy kid who was constantly distracted, wiggling his feet as if his shoes were on fire, made me feel useful to someone at last.

One day while I was trying to get him to learn a poem, I thought that although I'd been made to hate it from the depths of my being, Italian was actually a beautiful language. Reading it was like singing. If I hadn't automatically associated it with those swaggering fascists, maybe I'd have continued humming those songs I'd heard on Barbara's gramophone:

A kiss you'll get
If you come back
But there'll be no more
If you leave for war

and maybe Maja would have done the same, just like the farmers. Over time, the whole of this valley would have become a crossroads for people who could understand one another in more than one way, not some ill-defined spot in Europe where everyone scowled at each other. But Italian and German were walls that grew higher and higher. By now, the languages had become racial markers. The dictators had turned them into weapons and declarations of war.

7

An army jeep pulled up in front of the farm. Two soldiers helped him get out. His leg was in plaster and he was using crutches to support himself as he walked. After a few steps they picked him up under his arms and left him at the door. Erich hurried to assure me that he was not an invalid; only his leg had been wounded and when it healed he would immediately leave again for the front. The soldiers nodded.

When the jeep took to the road again, Erich asked after you, and when I shook my head he quickly changed the subject. He said, "It's not true that I'll go back to combat, Trina. I will never fight again. If they come back to look for me, I'll escape to the mountains," and he tried awkwardly to get up, anxious to see the house again. His face was drawn and there was a deep line, like a cut, on his forehead. I couldn't stop looking at him. I put a hand through his hair, which was sparse and had turned white blond. His ways, however, were the same as ever: fingers drumming on the table and a boyish hunger that made him devour four chunks of cheese in a couple of bites. Ma started cooking straight away, and without saying a thing she went out to buy a chicken. On her return, she found

Erich sleeping in the chair, chin on his chest. Michael came running   someone must have alerted him. He stood there watching Erich sleep, smiling, his head nodding. As if he were the father and Erich his son. Michael then went to wash in the bath. He combed his hair before the mirror and put on his dark jumper, the one for holidays. I washed too and combed my frizzy hair, putting the wooden stick through it. Ma laid the table with the white cotton cloth. We sent away the people from neighboring farms who came round asking to see the veteran.

"Tomorrow, tomorrow!" we begged, blocking them at the door.

He ate everything lopsided, resting his head in his hand. He kept asking me to pour some more wine; I had never seen him so set on drinking. Michael didn't stop asking questions, not even for a minute. Erich, annoyed, said he wanted to eat in peace: talking about the war made his stomach knot up. He grimaced in pain as he chewed and I realized that he was drinking to dull the pain in his leg.

When he went to the stables, he found the animals in a bad way. He said one of the cows had infected eyes and the sheep were malnourished.

"I don't want to fight anymore, Trina," he mumbled, caressing the cow's muzzle. "Never again."

When we were in bed he showed me his leg and the wound from which they'd taken a bullet. We stayed up late talking. Talking as if we no longer knew one another. That evening I didn't think of you, not even for a second.

*

When the pain eased, the first thing he did was walk to the construction site.

"Are you crazy?" I asked. "Do you want to go all that way?"

"You look after the animals today. I'll start tomorrow," he ordered.

He went off at a limp, moving like a pendulum. I felt sorry for him. When Michael joined him he found him staring slack-jawed at the ditches into which lorries were vomiting earth, his hands stuck through the iron cable fencing. The veins standing out on his skin made it look bluish. Michael kept to his side and stood there watching the laborers with him, the angry caterpillar trucks, the *carabinieri* smoking as they leaned against the hoods of their jeeps.

"Come, Papa, let's go."

While Michael pedaled, Erich, wedged between his forearms, looked at the firs covering the mountains and breathed in the scent of the sky.

When they got to the inn, he told Michael, "If they call me up again, I'll escape to the mountains."

"I don't want to fight with the Italians either, Papa."

"Not the Italians and not the Germans. I won't go to war again." He spoke angrily.

"But I'd actually like to fight for the Führer," Michael said.

"The Germans have become racist and bloodthirsty."

"The Führer must have his reasons for acting like that."

"What are his reasons for annihilating everyone?" Erich

went for him. "What's the reason for this war that's been dragging on for years? What's it got to do with us?"

"He'll bring about a better world, Papa."

"A world of servants doing the goose-step, that's what!"

"The Nazis won't build the dam. Doesn't that make you happy?" Michael continued, unperturbed.

At this Erich shouted once more, so loudly that the old men at the table in the inn turned to look at him.

"The fact that they won't annihilate us is not enough for me to approve what they're doing!" He got up clumsily. Michael tried to steady him, but Erich dodged his arm and grabbed his jumper, pulling Michael close. "You don't know it all. You're nothing but a thug," he said with disgust, "Go off and join Hitler, you idiot."

They didn't speak for days. That evening they put on an artificial cordiality in front of me but it only made them seem more hateful. After setting out the supper I sat between them, in Erich's place, and as I swallowed my soup I wondered why I'd gone to the trouble of raising children.

On evenings when Michael went out I'd reproach Erich, telling him to let it go — when it came down to it, Michael worked hard and handed over all the money he earned without batting an eyelash.

"Hitler or no, Michael is a good kid. You shouldn't be so hard on him." And I reminded him how long Michael had stood over him, watching him sleep when the Italian soldiers brought him back from the front. "Isn't his affection enough for you?" I asked angrily.

But when I talked like this Erich attacked me, exclaiming that having a child who was a Nazi was the worst thing that could have happened to him. The fact that people didn't understand, that almost everyone was like Michael, didn't make a particle of difference. Nazism was the greatest possible disgrace, and sooner or later the world would realize it.

The noise from airplanes arriving out of nowhere never stopped, yet now that Erich was with me again, the war went back to seeming unreal. I had no more time to think about it, and I remembered it only when a telegram arrived in the village to announce someone's death. Then you'd hear crying coming from the other farms. You'd see people showing up in procession, dressed in black and not knowing what to say, especially if it was a young boy who had died. On such days the bell rang for hours and hours. Erich didn't miss a single Mass now.

He quickly resumed his life as a farmer and dedicated himself to restoring the animals to health. He took them to new pastures where they could graze until they were full. He'd come back early and by mid-afternoon the animals were already back in the stables. Since there were fewer of them they weren't so squashed together. We'd had some of them slaughtered because we didn't have the money to take care of the entire herd. We were paid well for them because there wasn't much meat to be found now. According to Erich the old cows could be sold and with the younger ones we could raise veal calves.

After work he'd go out with his cigarette hanging from the side of his mouth. Sometimes he'd call Grau, and at the door he'd say to me, "Come."

"Wait for me to get ready."

"No, just come as you are."

And we'd argue because I no longer wanted to go out looking like a gypsy. I didn't want to be frumpy now that my husband was back from the war. So I would get ready in a hurry, but when I appeared with my hair combed, wearing my checked dress, he'd already be out, and I'd stand in front of the mirror and see how old I looked.

In the streets of Curon, Erich said to everyone he met, "We should sabotage the worksite before we're flooded."

But the old men answered that they were too old to do those things, and the few men who weren't at the front said nothing would happen anyway – Hitler would soon occupy the Tyrol and the dam wouldn't be mentioned again. Others said, "Hold your tongue, unless you want the Blackshirts to come and beat you up while you're asleep."

So Erich went round to the women, but they shook their heads and replied that somewhere in the world they had husbands or sons at the front, men who might still be alive or had perhaps been shot by machine guns. They had no space in their heads to think about the dam at the other end of the river, where they couldn't see it.

"God won't allow such a thing."

"Curon is the seat of the bishop."

"St. Anne will protect us."

Erich told me to shut up when I said that God is the hope of those who don't want to lift a finger.

8

Many died in Eastern Europe, others in Russia, on the banks of the Don. Telegrams were delivered constantly, the official handing them to the women looking at his boots and touching the peak of his cap before getting back on his scooter. The priest rang the death bell into the evening. The inn emptied and Erich said that the bodies wouldn't come home. We'd have to ask the *podestà* for a collective tombstone.

German soldiers arrived in the village with increasing frequency, declaring that the Reich would soon take over the South Tyrol. Some cheered; others gave them a wide berth.

Karl managed to get hold of a radio. The men would gather around to listen to it and he complained that no one ordered any beer, and he'd soon take a hammer to it. Erich went to the inn to listen to the radio and he reported to me that the Duce was making increasingly triumphalist proclamations, a sign that things were going badly.

"Papa, it won't be long before Hitler comes to liberate us," Michael said to him one evening.

Erich moved his plate to one side, looked straight at Michael and replied, "If you sign up with the Germans, don't set foot in this house again."

*

When the armistice was announced, people ran into the streets to cheer. And when the Führer's soldiers arrived, women leaned out of their windows with handkerchiefs and waved from the doorsteps. Men we'd never seen were now treated like liberators. We became the southern region of the Reich: the Pre-Alpine Operations Zone. Some said the fascists were still in command, others that they'd lost power. In the weeks to come, Italian employees were driven from their posts, but without a hair on their head being harmed. There were announcements about rehiring the locals, and Italian was forbidden in all public offices. All those who'd had qualifications or held posts taken by Mussolini were invited to show up to reclaim them.

From the moment the Nazis arrived, Erich stopped going out. He walked with his hands behind his back, and when I asked, "What do we do now?" he wouldn't answer. Not even when Michael came to tell him that the works at the dam had been halted – "the Führer wants to build railways" – not even then did Erich open his mouth.

Only when the Germans took complete control of the territory and people realized that Mussolini, whether prisoner or free, didn't matter anymore; only when the orders and dispatches coming thick and fast from the command centers in Merano announced the imminent conscription of men in fiery letters; only then did I understand what was agitating Erich. He knew, after seeing the Nazis killing and taking prisoners at the front, that having decided to stay in Curon and not leave for Germany at the time of the Option was a mistake he'd pay for. The Germans would first take aim at all those who'd stayed in '39. Those who hadn't put blind faith in Hitler from the start. Michael said the same. "We have to enrol as volunteers. We have to make up for our mistake."

One evening he took Erich aside and said quietly, "Listen, Papa. Hitler knows our history. He knows what we've been through. He'll enlist us, it's true, but not to send us to some far-off front. He'll send us somewhere close by, or he'll give us administrative tasks. Only those who don't spontaneously enroll will be sent to fight in Europe," he concluded, reaching for Erich's hand.

"What do you know about it?" Erich asked scornfully.

"I enlisted yesterday."

Erich's head shot up and Michael held his gaze.

"I did it for you, too, Papa."

Finally, one night when we couldn't sleep, Erich told me about the front.

"We marched for days without stopping. I saw the mountains in Albania, low and arid, but steep and full of crevices. We clambered along the mule tracks for entire nights and couldn't even ask if there was still a long way to go. I shot men – I couldn't say how many I killed. No more than anyone else, but enough to earn me a place in hell. All things considered, it's unfair that I'm still alive. We Tyroleans were often badly treated by the other soldiers. They made us clean their shoes, and no one ever called us by name. When we were sent to Greece, I made a friend, a guy from Rovereto. He fell sick with diphtheria as soon as he got there. Before inspection I'd prick my finger and rub a few drops of blood on his face to banish his pallor. I gave him a few more days of life. Then one evening they got me to smoke with him before they killed him, right in front of me. Two minutes later I had to eat rations."

I held my breath and rested my chin on my clasped knees. I looked at the moonlight coming through the window.

"And the Germans are more ferocious than the Italians. They deport, torture…" As I turned toward him he repeated, "Trina, if they intend to enroll me again I'll escape to the mountains."

"Then we'll escape together."

A few days later, Michael showed up in military uniform. He came to get a hug and he smiled contentedly, as if his clothes had finally made him a man.

"Soon I'll be made lieutenant or commander of the Wehrmacht, Mamma. I'll be paid well and have stars on my uniform." He was chuffed. I nodded but I didn't look at him as I straightened the lapels on his coat. "You're not happy with me either?" he asked, chin in the air.

"Don't worry about it. I'm never happy."

"This is a smart uniform, isn't it?"

"Yes, it's very smart."

He said he'd been assigned to a patrol unit in Val Padana. It was a mission against the partisans infesting northern Italy.

At the door I took him by the shoulders. "I'm going to ask you something now and you must say yes."

He looked at me, perplexed, and did not answer. I had to repeat it to him three times. Only then did he nod, inviting me to speak.

"You have to help us escape."

He paled. Clenched his fists.

"It's our secret," I said to him.

No answer.

"Say it: it's our secret."

He said it.

"If the Führer means more to you, you can expose us and have us shot. You can get revenge on your grandmother and take it out on your father," I went on, challenging him.

"Did he ask you to do this?"

"No, he doesn't know anything about it."

He narrowed his eyes and his face reddened. He looked at me the way you do an enemy, but at that moment his love no longer mattered to me. All I wanted was to protect Erich and escape with him.

"I'll come and tell you where it's safest," he said in a voice not his own, and he left without giving me a kiss. He went to Ma's room and kissed her. Then he walked past me in his gray coat and slammed the door. The candle on the sideboard went out.

I took out two bags. I put in Erich's heavy clothes, his rough wool jumpers, a scrap of soap, scarves, socks, a blanket. In what little space was left I would put a brick of polenta, tins of salted meat, crackers, dry biscuits. I would put a water bottle in my bag; in Erich's a flask of grappa. I prepared everything without thinking, as if it were suddenly clear to me that we had no other choice. I hid the bags in the trunk and threw some old rags over them.

I went to Ma's room. I shook her shoulder and sat down beside her.

"Are you all right?" she asked me.

"Yes, I'm okay."

"Michael will come home soon."

"Listen, Ma. Erich and I are going to escape into the mountains. If you want to come with us, you can, but it would be better for you to go and stay with Peppi."

"If your husband were to enlist, you could start teaching."

"I don't want to teach in a Nazi school. And anyway Erich won't enroll."

"They kill deserters' wives."

"They'll kill you too if you stay here. You must go to Peppi."

She asked me to leave her room. That evening she called me in and without looking up she declared, "Fine. I'll go to Peppi."

I heated water for the bath. When Erich came home I helped him to wash and put supper on the table. I tried not to meet his glance. Ma wanted to stay in her room and I took her a cup of broth.

"I've packed the bags. They're in the trunk."

He raised his head and nodded.

"Has Michael gone?"

I told him he had. His face registered his disgust though he kept on chewing listlessly. At that moment, I felt a new desire take hold of me, one I'd never felt before. I wanted to get rid of everything I had. My belongings, the animals, my thoughts. All I wanted was to fasten the straps and go. Get out of here.

I wrote a letter to Peppi, begging him to come and get Ma as soon as possible. I didn't think about Michael, though I knew I might never see him again. I didn't think about the war or the mountains that would hide us if we didn't die on them. I didn't think about you. Every evening for four years, I'd written to you in an old notebook. I reread it all in one go and then threw it in the fire. Scarlet embers veined the ashes, and the fire slowly worked its way through the pages. Crackling, coming to life. I had never felt so free.

9

One morning some men came to ask why I wasn't coming back to teach. They asked if I was opposed to the Nazi school.

"Absolutely not," I said.

I'd only just got rid of them when a car stopped outside the farm. Two officers asked for Erich Hauser. I had left the door open and the sun was shining through the house. My cardigan was unbuttoned and one of the officers looked me up and down, from my dressing gown to my calves.

"I'll send him to the barracks. Right now he's out with the animals."

"Why hasn't he enrolled as a volunteer?"

"Because of me," I replied. "I'm not well. We decided that our son would enlist and my husband would stay here. He's already fought for two years; he came back from Greece wounded."

They checked their list to see if Michael had really signed up and on finding his name they softened a little.

Erich went to the stables to kill the calf. He shot it with a pistol he'd brought back from the front. He skinned the animal and hung the meat up to drain. The cows kicked and bellowed loudly. They were scared for the whole day. Erich brought the meat into the house and I cut it up in pieces and put it in glass jars. A slice of meat, a handful of salt, just like that, until the meat was finished and so was the salt. He led the three cows to his friend Florian's farm, and left the sheep with another farmer called Ludwig. He asked them to keep them, making up an excuse. They would understand the next day. When he came back in the evening I started frying the meat in butter. I poured the fat over our polenta and we ate. We ate until we were sick. As I looked at the clusters of stars in the night sky, I lost the sense that any of this was real: our escape to the mountains, Ma's move to Peppi's in Sondrio. The fact that my son was a Nazi.

"I worry that they'll be angry with Michael," I said.

"I worry that Michael will send the Nazis after us."

"Stop saying such things. He won't do that."

"And they won't do anything to him apart from ask a few questions."

I cleared the table. Washed the dishes in the sink and cleaned the sideboard, the furniture, and finally the floor.

"Why are you wearing yourself out like that?" Erich asked. "They'll trash the farm from top to bottom, maybe even burn it. There's no point in leaving it clean."

"Well, I'll leave it clean anyway."

Erich shrugged and then put some more things in the bag. He made two sacks of straw for us to sleep in. I went from room to room, making sure everything was in order. I needed to believe we would be returning. That Ma would come back and do her knitting here again, needles at her armpits.

Everyone would come home. Peppi and his wife, Irene, the young boys from the village who'd been recruited by the Nazis, Michael, who'd be reconciled with Erich. And you, too, would come back. The war would be over, and they would bring you back to Curon at last.

We left in the middle of the night. I cast an eye over the kitchen and the dining room: tea towels folded and stacked, glasses still dripping. The smell of butchered meat lingered on the air.

There was a crescent moon on the Ortler. I undid Grau's chain. He lifted his head and looked at me with his wrinkled eyes. I stroked his muzzle and tail.

"See you soon, Grau." Erich rubbed his ears.

Then he took my hand and we went. I couldn't remember the last time he'd taken my hand. I felt soft and light.

We set off toward the larches. In the woods, the darkness suddenly grew denser and the cold was cutting. Erich put on his torch and stopped to look at my face in its light. Our mouths were spewing out fog.

"Are you frightened?" he asked me.

"No."

I wanted to kiss him there in the middle of the woods.

"It's best to climb now while it's dark. As high as we can, and walk toward Switzerland. There are caves and barns. We'll find shelters higher up. We should go higher than the Germans patrolling the borders, and stop before we meet the Swiss police."

When the climb was steep we kept silent. We had to listen for noises. Erich kept his pistol in his hand and the hunting gun over his shoulder. The constant rustling of branches brought to mind not soldiers, but snakes and lizards crackling over the leaves, wolves – who are frightened of noises – owls with yellow eyes. I pulled Ma's scarf over my nose, then covered my ears and finally my head.

When I tripped or the terrain was steep, Erich would hand me the torch and then scold me because I'd light up his face. We stopped for a moment to listen to the sound of a stream. We filled the water bottle. The water was ice-cold and I told Erich to drink slowly. I wanted to talk, but he wasn't paying attention. The silence was profound, like the silence that must have been pooling in our empty house.

"Keep your ears pricked. From here on out we may meet wolves."

"Erich, when will it be light?"

"Not long now."

10

Light, first pink, then blue, pierced the pitch-dark sky. The sun came up. Erich pointed to Curon, looking tiny so far below us. We sat on the rocks and ate crackers with cheese. He had me take a sip of grappa and I choked it down. A clear glow now illuminated the plain; branches and shrubs jutted out from the cliffs. I felt like I was on top of the world. Like I'd left it and didn't belong there anymore.

"We can settle down here," said Erich.

There was a cave on the side of the mountain, so narrow you had to crawl to get into it. Erich inspected it and said it wasn't an animal's den. We started gathering branches and trampling down the remnants of snow.

"Will we have to camp in there?" I asked him, feeling uncertain.

"Only for a few days, and then we'll go to a farm where they'll put us up."

"Who will put us up?"

"Father Alfred gave me a note to present to the lady who owns the farm. Her son is a young priest in Malles." He took out the note he had in his pocket.

I looked around. "Will we have to sleep on the ground?"

"Let's go and get some leaves. We'll stuff our mattresses," he answered patiently. "Our sacks will help keep out the cold."

I wouldn't let him wander more than a meter away from me. I threatened to scream or go back to the valley if he did. I didn't want to be on my own for any reason at all. Erich caressed my head and explained that he'd soon have to hunt some hares or birds, or ask the farmers to sell him some cheese. There was no sense in going together. He handed me the pistol, and he kept the rifle. I had never fired a weapon before and I didn't try now, because there were only six bullets in the cylinder.

"Just use every bit of your strength when you press the trigger," he said.

I stared at the iron barrel, heavy in my cold hands. We went to gather leaves and then we surveyed the area. There wasn't a soul about. When we got back, Erich was convinced: "No one will come this far up."

"But the snow will come."

"Yes, there'll be a lot of it."

"So what will we do then?"

"We'll only have to hold out for a few days, Trina, to make sure that the Germans won't be crossing this road. Then we'll stay at the farm, and repay their hospitality by working. We'll give them whatever money we have."

"Will the war end in the meantime?"

"I hope so."

We took off our shoes in the midday sun and ate more cheese. Erich slept first. I took the pistol and went outside the cave to look at the light sparkling in the sky, the long narrow clouds chasing after each other in that immaculate blue. I saw an eagle circling in the distance. I walked by the trees, examining them. Kicked a few stones. The air was still.

"If you see tree trunks with scratches, get out of there. It means there's a wolf around," Erich had warned me.

"What if he's right in front of me?" I asked nervously.

"You have to shoot him between the eyes. Same with the Germans. And the Italians. If you want to survive, you always shoot between the eyes."

"We haven't escaped the war up here," I said to Erich one evening in front of the fire. "This pistol is the war."

He nodded. "But we haven't become their accomplices."

When darkness climbed up the mountain, I'd sit and look at the sky, trying to keep the light in it as if it were the last of some milk, and I was a ravenous infant. But everything would go black and desolate an instant later, and you couldn't even see the shapes of the trees. I'd go back into the cave defeated, put my head in my hands and choke back sobs. Erich let me be. Sometimes he'd come close and try to hug me but I told him that I didn't want his hugs. I just wanted the sun to rise.

When the light returned I soon forgot about the unsettling darkness, and as I looked around, I dreamed with open eyes. I was a young bride who'd come up the mountain for love of her adventurous husband. I was a guerrilla fighter feared by the Germans. A teacher who'd brought her children to safety.

In the afternoons, when the hours dragged, we leaned against a tree and spoke of things we'd never mentioned before.

"I wonder where Marica is," Erich said one day, blowing into his hands.

I froze as if I'd seen a wolf and moved closer to him. He hadn't spoken your name for so long. He repeated his sentence, and said the time when we couldn't speak about it was over.

"I just want her to be well and safe, and I hope the war hasn't done anything to her."

"Don't you want to see her again?"

"I don't think that will happen."

"What about your sister?"

"Yes, I'd like to see her again."

"Would you really?"

"Yes, to ask why."

"That's all you'd like to ask?"

"Yes, Trina. That's all."

11

I lost track of the days. I asked Erich when we'd leave for the farm. He replied that it wasn't time yet, and I'd fall into a temper because I wanted to get out of there. When I asked him how we'd know how the war was going, he'd laugh and tell me that not even two weeks had gone by.

The salted meat soon ran out. The polenta and the crackers too. The cheese ran out, the biscuits ran out. Erich would disappear for hours. I was alone on that mountaintop. I looked at the valley and felt a strange dizziness, a break in the wind that stopped me in my tracks. He managed to get a slice of speck or a piece of cheese from the farmers, but we were eating less and less and his face was yet more skeletal, hollow under his scruffy beard. He caught marmots, still as statues, striking them between the shoulders with a stick. They were a feast, those marmots. We lit the fire and roasted the meat, which we ate right down to the bone. I felt yet more feral, but not inhuman, like I had while he was at the front.

One morning while Erich was out hunting, I began wandering along the riverbank. I deluded myself into thinking that I might find some fish, but I barely managed to fill the canteen with shards of ice. I knocked at the door of a farmhouse, and I told the woman who opened the door that we were deserters trying to get to Switzerland. I got a can of soup and a flask of wine. I swore I would return to pay for them, and I headed back toward the cave feeling victorious, imagining Erich's blue lips smiling at me in satisfaction. "One less day now," he'd say with his mouth full, and we'd drink the wine, relishing the feeling of it hitting our stomachs.

I slowly climbed up through the trees. My steps sank into the dry snow as if it were old salt. I thought about Erich shoveling it; it was part of our daily struggle. I heard voices. German voices, bombarding someone with questions. Aggressive, shouting. There were ten steps between me and the cave. I stretched so I could see. The soldiers had their backs to me and were repeating obsessively, "Partisan? Deserter?" Erich didn't answer. I crouched down. Two birds stared at me from the branches above. I lay on my stomach in the snow. The cold numbed my breasts. I could see them clearly now. They continued to interrogate Erich and he remained mute. I took out the pistol. There were only six bullets. I squeezed it with all my strength. I aimed at the back of the first one, and he fell with a dull thud. The other turned at once and I shot him in the chest. He let out a strangled cry. I kept shooting at those bodies lying there until there were no more bullets in the pistol. Erich, paralyzed, had his back to the rock, and his stony eyes stared at my face without recognition. I shook him as if he were a snow-laden branch and growled between my teeth for him to move. So he helped me to grab the Germans' weapons. One for me, one for him. We got their blood on us. We searched their coats and pocketed the banknotes we found. One of their wallets was full of marks. With that money we could buy something to eat in the farmers' houses and pay for their hospitality at the farm. We dragged the bodies into the cave. I threw the empty pistol on the bodies and we covered them with snow. The snow that fell overnight and in the coming days would bury them forever.

We went higher, marching with the quick step of the assassin. The snow we were trampling and in which we left our prints was sticky and heavy. We gripped the pistols. Our hearts pummeled our chests.

"There are other prints," Erich said. "They must have come from up here."

We changed direction. We marched in silence. When we came across animal tracks or bootprints we'd change course. Our hands were cracked with frostbite.

"Where are we?" I asked when the sun slipped behind the mountain.

"The Swiss border is over there."

"And the farm? Where is this farm?" I cried, exasperated.

"It can't be far," Erich said, lost.

Our legs wouldn't carry us any longer. I was sure that we'd be dead in the next few hours. When I threw myself on the ground, Erich ordered me to get up immediately and not to stop walking for any reason.

"If we stop we'll freeze to death."

There were no more trees. There was nothing else on the distant ridges, just snow.

"Look over there!" Erich said. He didn't have the energy to shout.

In the middle of all that white was a tiny stone construction. We went closer. It was a circular chapel, with a cross rising from its pointed roof, planted there like a feather.

We didn't hear any voices coming from inside. Erich opened the door. Three men jumped to their feet. They shouted something in German. A shot rang out.

"Don't shoot!" I screamed.

We raised our hands, still holding the pistols, which had become an extension of our bodies.

"We're not soldiers! We're not Nazis and we're not fascists!" I shouted.

They exchanged glances.

"Are you deserters?" one of them asked, lowering his gun.

We nodded. They ordered us to put away our pistols. We asked them to do the same. I might have looked like a tramp, but my face reassured them.

I will never forget those three. The father, with an ambivalent expression on his goaty face, a squashed nose and thick lenses that made his face smaller. His sons, pale and shocked. They made me think of Michael. They were fleeing the Germans, while Michael was after anyone who was against the Nazis. If he had gone into that chapel he would have killed them. Or they him.

They were eating bread without salt. They were about to

light a fire and Erich helped. With the flames crackling, the walls of the chapel seemed to come to life, and like a coward, I thanked God because now I was warm.

I took out the can of soup and the flask of wine and set them by the fire. "Have you seen any soldiers?"

"The Germans know there are deserters hiding out around here, near the border," said the blond boy, drinking his wine.

"You have to be careful not to go too far over the summit. The Swiss police are arresting deserters every day," the other boy put in.

They told us the war was turning out badly for Hitler. The Russian campaign was a complete disaster. Thousands were dead in Stalingrad and the city's cellars were full of the wounded, abandoned to fate. They told us they were trying to get to Bern, where they had relatives who would protect them. They were from Stelvio. The sons had taken advantage of a leave to escape, and the father hadn't shown up at recruitment. Like Erich, he had fought in the Italian ranks, after which he didn't want to hear another thing about war. The mother had died some years before.

"If she had been alive, she would never have left her village, and the Nazis would have arrested her or maybe shot her on our account," said the littlest one.

I said nothing. I looked at them and felt disgust – with them, with the Nazis, with my son. Disgust, mixed with a desire to have Michael beside me, to warm our hands together before the fire.

"The Germans have been here. It's not a good idea to stay,"

the father said again. "You'll have to climb up higher to wait out the war. You'll find other deserters. There are shelters and barns up there."

"It isn't any colder there than it is here," the blond boy reassured us.

They offered us chicory coffee, and that bitter sludge was so good I wanted to dunk my face in it. They gave Erich some tobacco; he didn't have any more and he was so happy with that crumpled cigarette that he held the smoke in his lungs for as long as he could. One of the boys drained his cup and went to the door with his pistol.

"After three hours I'll change places with you," said his brother, still seated.

I woke up next morning with the blond boy nestled against my shoulder. We carved some discs out of branches and put them under our shoes so we could walk in the snow. Erich made the branches flexible, working them with his knife, and I bound them with string, cutting it off the ball with my teeth. We made some for them too. Before going they left us a hunk of their tasteless bread. The father repeated that we should climb further, and not be afraid of the cold. Then he and his sons left without saying goodbye, going in the opposite direction to ours. We watched them grow smaller against the white.

It went on snowing and we put on all the socks we had. I thought of Ma, and how she'd say that cold feet mean you're cold all over. I often thought of her. I could see her, sitting and sewing in the badly stuffed chair. I never had any idea what was going round in her head.

When I turned to look at the chapel with the crucifix, the snow was already heaped against the door. It was impossible to get in now. I thought about the bodies of the two Germans I'd killed. There was nothing around us but white, and the sound of the wind.

12

We walked for hours in the deadly cold, and the snow made its way into our open shoes. When it stopped snowing, we forced ourselves to eat some bread. While we were eating, Erich suddenly leaped to his feet and pointed to two men in the distance. He stuffed the bread in his pocket and ran breathlessly, yelling at the top of his voice, "Hey, you!," tripping with every step, his shrieks dying out in that white desert. Buckled under the damned bag, I couldn't keep up with him. I wanted to fall down and die.

"Erich, stop!" I shouted.

But he kept on running, plunging his stick into the ground until it cracked and he stumbled.

"Erich, we're not going to catch up with them. Stop!" I yelled again.

He came back panting and warned me, "We have to follow their tracks, Trina, before the snow erases them. Those men are local farmers and they can tell us which way to go."

In fact, the footprints led us to the farm. We stopped and leaned on our sticks to study it. We knelt down and waited for our breath to calm. I could feel my tears freezing.

A woman came to the door and started shoveling. Erich

pushed me forward. I took out the note from Father Alfred. I could feel my legs ready to collapse under me, as if my frozen feet wouldn't be moving again. I said hello in the voice of an apologetic child. The woman was fat, with bristly disheveled hair. One look was all she needed to tell her we were deserters.

"Father Alfred sent us, the priest of Curon," I told her. She didn't answer. "We've fled the war. We're dying of cold," I went on, handing her the note. She didn't even look at it.

She shouted out a name, never taking her eyes off me. An old man came through the door shouldering a rifle. Another man appeared, and yet another in a priest's cassock. A woman came out holding a girl by the hand. Erich walked forward, hands in the air. It continued to snow on us. Nothing is more pitiless than the falling snow.

There was a fire burning inside the farmhouse. Mattresses leaned against the walls of the single room. The floor sloped so much that it made me dizzy to walk on it. My skin felt tight, and being watched by those six people made me uneasy. It seemed like the warmth from the flames would burn my cheeks. Even if I'd wanted to keep my sobs back, I knew I could no longer do it.

"Are you Nazis?" asked the middle-aged man.

"No."

"Fascists?"

"We're not fascists."

"We're not Nazis or fascists!" Erich declared, vexed. "We're not anything, just farmers. I don't want to fight this war anymore."

"We're friends of Father Alfred, the priest of Curon," I repeated.

Finally the priest smiled. The fat woman handed him the note. After he read it he took our hands, embraced Erich and welcomed us. We could help out by finding food and repairing the stables, though there weren't any more animals. The fat woman had sold them at a fair, convinced that you needed money during war.

"But money isn't worth anything during a war," the priest concluded with a sigh.

"We're friends from the village," said the old man's daughter. "We escaped from Malles a few weeks ago."

"We'll give whatever we have in rent," Erich broke in. "We know it's a sacrifice for you."

The fat woman nodded and invited us to come closer. I was overwhelmed with sleepiness and wanted to be alone. The cold inside didn't even seem that cold to me. The women smiled when I told them, "If you need a frying pan I've got one in my bag. I climbed all the way up here with the handle sticking into my back."

The fat woman laughed and then pointed to the door that led behind the house. "If soldiers come, you have to go out that way. We're the last farm left. They're not looking for any other dwellings. A few kilometers from here, Switzerland begins."

"Where should we go if they come?"

"To the east. Go back down the mountainside until you get to a row of pines. There are some barns there."

We returned to the fire. The middle-aged couple looked us over from head to foot. Their daughter, Maria, was mute, and she stared at us the whole time with ragdoll eyes.

"We'll keep watch just for tonight. You can take a turn tomorrow, after you've rested," the old man said to Erich.

13

It was raining next morning. The priest put his hands together and prayed, wrapped in his black habit, which made me feel melancholy. His mother bustled about with her back to us. Every now and then she'd say to him, "You made a mistake becoming a priest. You should have married Francesca."

Patiently he'd reply, "Mamma, I married God."

He had narrow shoulders and thinning hair. An ageless face. Eyes as black as that melancholy black habit.

"Can priests desert too?" I asked him.

He gave me the same compassionate smile before saying that he hadn't deserted, only refused to obey the Nazis.

"Hitler is a heathen. The priests who have supported him aren't worthy of Christ," he said in his calm voice.

He told me that Maria's father would go hunting and stop by a farmer who always left something out for him. A couple of sausages, some cheese. Since their daughter had gone mute, not even the parents spoke much. Once every ten days, two of his cousins would leave him a sack of polenta and some eggs at a secret location in the mountains. He also told me that none of them could return to Malles until the end of the war.

"Will the war end soon?" I asked. He opened his hands but said nothing.

Erich went outside and sat talking to the old man. Then he busied himself cleaning the stables, repairing the mangers, replacing planks of wood that had rotted under the weight of the snow. I asked the fat woman how I could help. And in a gentle voice, she said I should simply think about resting for now. She asked me to tell her a little about my life before the war. So I told her how I'd studied to become a teacher but the fascists hadn't let me teach, and I'd also worked as a farmer, and in the end we'd escaped up here one night because my husband had decided to desert.

"We'll get ourselves killed tagging along with the men," she commented, pointing her chin toward her son, who was praying again.

Outside, the sky was clear, and the snow reflected a flat light. The white left no room for anything else. The fat woman mixed the polenta and braised an onion in my frying pan. I was happy that she was using it.

"Last week they came back with a chamois, another time a pheasant. We ate meat even on Friday," she said with satisfaction. "Who knows if they'll find more? I really like meat."

"We had to eat it quickly since animals scent it," the priest added. "We do the night watch for them more than for the Germans. We can't do anything against the Germans."

"Will they come up here?" I asked.

He opened his arms again and his mother gave me an apologetic look. "It's pointless asking priests questions. All they do is open their arms," she muttered. "Even as a child he was always opening his arms. Someone took his toys, beat the holy hell out of him and instead of reacting, he'd open his arms."

We ate together around an old table laid with care by the priest. We couldn't even look at our plates before the blessing: "Lord, bless the food we're about to eat and give some to all the families in the world," was his prayer. After our meal, the old man would retire to polish his rifle. He told us repeatedly that he'd killed dozens of Italians with that gun in the First World War.

"I'm Austrian for as long as I have this rifle," he'd say.

Erich and Maria's father went outside to smoke, watching the sky turn red, then black. Erich appreciated the company and the silence. The rest of us sat drinking glasses of hot water the fat woman made for us; according to her it prevented indigestion. We imagined the end of the war. I said I couldn't wait to start teaching and Maria's mother encouraged me, saying I must have been a good teacher. The priest didn't have any dreams. All he wanted was to go back to his church and say Mass again. When we talked about our hopes, he'd smile tactfully and I found myself wanting to tell him about you. Even the fat woman had a dream. She wanted to be a grandmother with a houseful of grandchildren.

We let ourselves get swept away by these fantasies while we drained our cups, curling our fingers around them until they were cold and pretending that there was still hot water in them. When the men came back in, silence fell over us and brought us back to earth, and we looked at each other sheepishly, as if we'd sinned by dreaming for so long.

Erich and Maria's father went out early in the morning looking for farmers' houses and offering to lend a hand. They gathered hay in cloths, loaded it onto their shoulders and took it to the stables. With any luck, they got slices of speck, pieces of cheese and a few liters of milk, which made me happy. Maria, too. If it wasn't snowing they went hunting. Sometimes they ran into herders dragging a few cows along and sleeping in the hay at night; more often, other deserters. If they managed to overcome their suspicion, they'd exchange news, which they'd pass on to us at table. Whenever they left, the old man would take up his rifle and stand sentinel at the doorway with a nasty look. He never ate at table with us; he'd stand, holding tight to his tin plate. He didn't pray, either. He ate hurriedly and then said he had to go and look outside to see what the weather was doing. He'd stay for hours studying the sky, patient as an astronomer.

I helped with the cooking only when they came back with meat, since the fat woman preferred not to have anyone else in the kitchen. When we saw the men coming back with part of an animal, just one person would stand guard in the mountain hut. Even the priest, after blessing the meat, would get busy skinning it. We'd set planks on the ground and leave it to drain for the whole day. We women would see to the butchering. Salting the meat made me think of our house, and I wondered whether the Germans had burned it down or given it to someone else.

Maria watched us with absent eyes, never lifting a finger to help. She had ash-blond hair and long, thin hands. She was the image of her mother, who was always at home with the old man, watching me in an off-putting way.

Every day, I'd open the door hoping the snow had melted. I wanted to touch the green grass, the silver rocks, the stony earth. Yet even when spring arrived, I saw only pure white, which disappointed me. I'd listen to the thud of the snow falling from the fir trees and then turn back inside. I'd ask the priest what day it was and he'd patiently reply with a saint's name. He said praying was the best way to wait out the war. So I knelt down with him and listened to him repeat the same prayer dozens of times.

One evening, I found a notebook and pencil he'd left for me under the bag I used as a pillow. I believe that diary was my salvation from the standstill of war. I filled its pages with letters. At first I wrote to Maja, long pages of recollections of our years along the Resia riverbank, studying for our high school diplomas and eating spoonfuls of Ma's cream on Wednesdays. Then I started writing to Barbara. At the end of every letter I asked if her sister had given her my note and I signed off swearing I would never forget how we used to lie on the grass or sit in the branches like swallows. I asked Erich to help me send them, but he laughed and said there was no way to post letters: we were on top of a mountain.

Since we'd been at the farm, Erich had lost his cadaverous look and had finally cut off his shaggy beard, looking into a shard of mirror that hung on the wall. He enjoyed spending time with Maria's father, going hunting with him and struggling to replace the rotten wood in the stables. The priest and the fat woman said that they had benefited from having someone like Erich around, and when we gave them money for rent, they gave some of it back. Sometimes he and Maria's father didn't find anything, and they'd come back chewing tobacco. Even if we drank only hot water or ate a slurry of cooked grass at those meals, I was glad he had a friend.

When summer came, they went down to the riverbank and came back with some hapless small fish the fat woman and I threw on the grill. I'd eat them, holding my breath so I wouldn't notice the rancid taste they left in my mouth.

After the morning prayer the priest would try to get Maria to pray too. Once I joined them, and as he prayed I thought how lucky he was to believe that the disaster of war and the perpetual nearness of death was part of God's plan. To my eyes, it was just proof that as far as God was concerned it was better not to exist. I was on the verge of confiding in the priest about you so many times – how beautiful you were, how proud – and telling him about the night you fled. But the thought that he would reply, "God only gives great sorrows to those who can bear them," as I'd once heard him say, held me back.

After prayers I'd ask Maria if she wanted to sit with me outside the farmhouse. Her parents would approach her and caress her face, repeatedly begging her to "Go with Trina," as if she were leaving on a long journey. When we were alone, I'd show her heaps of white rock and a few scattered pines, slashes of dark earth opening up where the snow was slowly melting, lonely gorges dotted with birches, birds soaring with outspread wings, heedless of bombs or soldiers. When she was with me, Maria had the carefree eyes of a child rather than vacant ones. She pointed out everything she saw: an eagle flying through a cloud, the polished stones of the riverbed. She liked to hear the snow crunch under her shoes. She nodded "yes" or shook her head "no," and let me put my hands through her ash-blond hair, which her mother washed with care now that the sun was back. I spent endless days with her and it was difficult to find any meaning in them. Every now and again I called her Marica. On rainy days we stayed inside the farmhouse and Maria drew in my notebook: thick-maned horses, long-haired dogs.

"Are you drawing because you don't know how to write?" I asked her.

I took her hand and guided it as she wrote her name. When she saw the letters she was forming, Maria broke out laughing.

"Can you remember now?"

She nodded in astonishment and took my hand excitedly, begging me to write more. I pointed to the pines, the clouds, the sun, and then I got her to write those words on a piece of paper. She made a drawing beside them and within a few days we had created a little book of ABCs, which she proudly showed to her parents and her grandfather.

When I told her I was tired, she'd go and kneel in the snow, then stand up and look with satisfaction at the dents in the white. Watching her from inside the chalet, I was seized by a strange desire to cry.

At night, lying on my bed of leaves, I resisted sleep because I thought I'd dream about you. But in fact I almost always dreamed about the blond boy who had fallen asleep against my shoulder; he woke me up shouting, "Trina, the war is over!"

Sometimes I'd say to Erich, "We'll live here our whole lives, and then one day when we least expect it, a German or an Italian will come and shoot us in the back."

He'd sigh, thrust his fists in his pockets and change the subject. "Tomorrow I'm going to see a farmer to get some cheese. Then we'll take a walk by ourselves."

And yet we never walked by ourselves, because he'd start talking to the priest and I liked having Maria near me. I'd have liked it if the fat woman had come with us, because she cheered me up. "C'mon, we're not dead yet!" she'd say, laughing when nostalgia got the better of me.

14

At the end of '44 the German reprisals intensified. What little news arrived concerned burned farms, the deportation of deserters, families of draft evaders thrown in prison. So the men decided to stand guard two at a time. Erich and the priest, the old man and Maria's father.

It was the latter who saw them coming. A January day in '45. A group of five soldiers bundled up in coats and wearing snowboots. The sun had only just come out and we were already up because the fat woman said we should take advantage of the few hours of light, so she woke us by clapping her hands. The priest was the only one who rose before her. He slept less than the rest of us and I hadn't seen him in bed once in over a year. He was the last to go to bed and when I opened my eyes he was already wearing his habit.

The fat woman was heating the leftover barley coffee, the priest was in front of the fireplace stoking the fire. All at once the old man opened the door. "The Germans! Germans!" he yelled gruffly. The fat woman dropped her saucepan.

"Did they see you?"

"They didn't, but they'll be here in a few minutes!"

"There are biscuits and crackers in the sack hanging on the door!" she shouted, pushing us out of the back door. "Everyone leave at once! Go east. There are barns beyond the row of pines."

"What about you?" asked the priest.

"I'll join you there."

The old man walked effortlessly through the powdery snow and ordered us to form two groups. He pushed ahead with his own – composed of Maria and her parents – and advised us not to lose sight of each other and to be prepared to shoot. Occasionally Erich turned around to make sure the soldiers weren't following us, and he'd exchange signs of understanding with Maria's father. After only a few steps my legs felt heavy. I worried that those beasts were mistreating the fat woman – or maybe they'd already killed her. Such thoughts made me want to shoot someone again.

At one point the priest halted and asked us to stop and pray. The old man told him not to spout nonsense. So the priest came up to me and told me that he knew those mountains like the back of his hand because he and his sister had climbed them with his father.

"Is your mother coming?"

"If they leave her alive, she'll come. She's grown heavy but she's still got strong legs."

When we got to the barn the old man ordered us to say "Peace!" out loud, so anyone inside could hear us. Erich pointed to some large footprints on the ground. The Germans had been here too. The barn was in fact empty, the roof partially collapsed, the door forced open. On the ground were pallets stuffed with rotten leaves and scattered stalks of hay.

"They started searching at the top," said Maria's father. "If they find us, they'll kill us."

"They won't find us," the old man replied, silencing him. "By now they're already back down in the valley."

We entered the barn one at a time. We squeezed together like rabbits, and Maria's father held his daughter's hands in his own. We kept quiet. When evening came the priest again asked us to pray and we indulged him, repeating his words distractedly. Maria looked at me with her empty eyes.

The fat woman arrived in the morning, walking slowly with a sly smile on her chapped lips. Thoughts of death, which we hadn't been able to put to rest despite our exhaustion, vanished in an instant.

"God helped you get all the way here!" exclaimed the priest as he ran toward her.

"What do you mean, God? It was these old legs!" she laughed.

The rest of us ran to embrace her too, and she set down the few things she'd managed to bring with her. A handful of grass to cook, a piece of *lardo*, a sack of polenta and a flask of wine.

"Don't kid yourselves. This will last today only, tomorrow at most."

She came into the barn and even with all that squalor she didn't seem dejected. She said we definitely wouldn't die of cold. I looked at her and forced myself to smile. I envied her her pluck more than I did the priest his faith.

"The Germans were looking for you," she told her son in a reproving tone. "If you'd married Francesca, none of this would have happened."

"I married God, Mamma," the priest said to her.

"They checked to see if I was hiding deserters. They turned out the drawers and cupboards," she said again, sipping from the flask of wine, which she then passed around. "But they didn't believe me," she finished, dispirited. "When they saw the mattresses against the wall they swore they'd be back."

We sat looking at one another, not talking, and to chase the thought away, she cut everyone a chunk of *lardo*. "Before getting out of the house, they ransacked the sideboard and pocketed what little there was. Luckily they didn't notice the sacks of polenta. Tomorrow one of you will go and get them and you'll tell us if we can go back," she wound up, chewing the *lardo*.

"Do you think they'll come back?" Erich asked her.

"I hope they croak!" she replied.

With the fat woman there, I thought less about my fear. Maybe by being around her I would end up like that one day. Maternal with strangers and unconcerned about things, whether the house, food or the warmth of the fire.

When they'd eaten the *lardo*, Erich and Maria's father went out to cut firewood. The old man took up his place by the door, his rifle pointed at the slope we'd come down the night before.

The fire struggled to stay alight because the branches we'd managed to gather were damp with frost. The barn filled up with so much smoke it made us cough.

★

At dawn the old man left alone for the farm.

"I'll come with you," Maria's father said with his sullen look.

"Stay here. There's no sense in both of us dying at the same time."

He came back after nightfall. In the dark we heard "Peace" repeatedly, before the broken door opened. He came in with his heavy tread and without a word went to sit down by his granddaughter. He put down his rifle and rubbed his hands over the flames.

"The farmhouse and the stables are gone. The bastards burned them down."

15

We camped out in the barn for nearly three months. Maria was always feverish and I would dream of finding her dead on the stale hay. We had become bony and emaciated, with gaunt faces. The only good thing was that our exhaustion left no room for fear. We ate a few juniper berries, cooked grass, little else. We went without food for days at a time. The cousins had less and less polenta to leave out for us. We got a dollop per head out of it at lunch and supper, and then we were once more at the mercy of whatever the men could scare up. There wasn't a single farmer willing to sell a hunk of meat or cheese. Those who'd survived the reprisals wouldn't let a soul come near, and even if you waved a wad of banknotes under their nose, they'd say that an old hen was worth more than that.

At the end of April, Maria's father and Erich went to see the cousins. If you had to die, better to be shot in the head than gnawed by hunger or devoured by wolves. We could no longer live without some way of counting the days, some time frame to cling to in order to keep going. Day after day, the rest of the world was erased from memory.

That time, the cousins gave them some sugar and a flask of

cider in addition to the polenta. Best of all, they said that the war was winding down.

"The Americans are liberating the whole of Europe. Hitler is about to fall. It's only a matter of time, and maybe not much!" they announced. "Stay strong. Next time you can come with us!"

We spotted Erich and Maria's father on their way back, passing the flask between them. They were laughing behind their scraggly beards. We all embraced one another in the barn, and the old man raised his rifle in the air. The fat woman put some water on to boil and declared that she would make some sweet polenta to celebrate.

"We'll each get a big spoonful!" she exclaimed with enthusiasm, weighing the sack in both hands.

"Can I help you?" I asked.

"Go and walk around a little with Maria – it'll do you both good."

The girl was at the door, looking at me like a dog. We headed for the pines. Erich and the priest walked behind us; they too were intent on imagining going home. Maria looked pretty with the scarf I'd given her round her neck. Looking at her, I thought that you might resemble her.

We had agreed not to vary the route of our walks. That way, at least, if one of us should fail to return, we'd know where to look. When we got to the familiar creekbed, we gathered fresh leaves, as we always did, to refresh the pallets we slept on. Maria challenged me to a joust, with branches for swords. I'd become her playmate. That morning our walk took longer than usual. The sun was high in the sky when we returned. As usual, we were hungry and Maria twisted her finger in her cheek to show how much she was looking forward to her sweet polenta.

In the barn, the body of the fat woman was sprawled like that of a carefree child on the floorboards, which had cracked under her weight when she fell. Blood poured slowly from her neck, making strange patterns on the ground. The old man, riddled with bullets, was still holding his rifle; his daughter's hand lay on his chest. They'd killed Maria's father as he lay asleep on the old leaves that we would have replaced with the fresh ones we'd gathered. His blanket was soaked with blood.

The priest said Mass that evening, and I went away so I wouldn't have to hear it. While he was speaking, I took the pistol and kept watch outside the door. I'd scented the odor of blood again, the desire to kill.

We took turns digging the grave. We laid the bodies one on top of the other, because we lacked the strength to dig four graves.

During the nights to come, even the priest shouldered a rifle, and he didn't kneel anymore when he prayed. I think he, too, had smelled blood. Maria slept beside me. I told her fairytales about gulls and the sea, which I'd never been to. I begged her to swallow a few spoonfuls of the sweet polenta the fat woman had cooked, but she obstinately refused.

We said nothing. Absolutely nothing, until Erich went back to the secret place where the cousins would leave provisions. On that day in May, they told us we could come out. The war was over.

Part Three

The Water

1

We descended the mountain, planting our feet firmly on the ground, which with every step became greener and lighter under the sun. I held Maria's hand firmly in mine. We left behind us the cold, the still-falling snow, our friends in their grave. Erich walked ahead of us and the priest kept the old man's rifle over his shoulder. It no longer repulsed him. On one of the last nights, I'd heard him fidgeting in his sleep. Like everyone else's, his peace was over.

When we got to the valley where all the paths converged, the priest stopped and said, "We're going over there. We'll carry on to Malles."

Maria freed her thin fingers from my hand and looked at me one last time with her wondering eyes.

"She'll stay with me. She'll keep the church tidy, ring the bell. I'll take care of her," he said.

We watched them disappear into the dense woods. A strange light fell through the leaves.

We went down in silence, Erich and I, alone, the same way we'd come up. I held his hand until Curon appeared. When we got through the forest we looked around cautiously, not sure if we should put our guns in our pockets or keep our fingers on the trigger. The clouds had vanished and the sky was one vast expanse of intense blue. The light was cheerful. There were people out in the streets, as if the war were a nightmare dispelled by the day. I thought I smelled warm bread.

When I saw our house my legs started to run. I wanted to open up the windows right away, to let air that wasn't war air into the rooms. At the door, I turned to look at the village. The animals were in the middle of the valley and at the edge of the woods, the wagons for transporting the new hay were the same as always. Erich looked at me, his eyes red with weariness, his beard prickly and gray.

Sprawled in a chair, a spent cigarette between his fingers: that's how we found Michael. You might have thought he was waiting for death. On the table there was some tobacco and a little picture of the Führer, creased and ruined.

"Should I leave?" he asked without looking at us.

"Get rid of that photo," Erich ordered.

Michael handed it to me and finally raised his head.

"He's dead," he said, pointing to Hitler.

His skin was drawn and his shoulders sagged. His clothes smelled of diesel.

"I couldn't come to tell you which way to go. They made me leave at night."

"Go and change now," I said.

Erich was already asleep. He hadn't even removed his filthy clothes. He slept for two days straight. I brushed away the fleecy spiders' webs hanging in all the corners, the dead flies stuck on the glass, and went out to buy bread and milk on credit. I wanted hot milk so badly. I went to Florian's farm and to Ludwig's to ask if they were still alive, and if the animals we'd left with them were still alive. Miraculously, they were.

I took the cows and the sheep to the fountain and then led them to the stables. I chased the mice with my broom, went to get some bags of hay. There were wounded men in the streets. Missing legs, arms, eyes. Their faces were unrecognizable. They leaned on their crutches and I turned my head away, ashamed of having survived. They'd spent the war with bombs falling on them or behind machine guns; Erich and I before the fat woman's fire. Some were celebrating victory by drinking beer in the street. Some talked about beating up the few who, having gone to the Reich in '39, had now come back to Curon, heads bowed, stateless. At the inn, some were swearing because we were still Italian. The Austrian empire no longer existed. Nazism had not saved us. And even if fascism was finished, we'd never be the same as before.

I wanted to go and embrace Maja, but at the same time, to stay hidden, because I wasn't the same Trina as before. I'd eaten ice to quench my thirst. I'd shot a man in the back. I gathered my courage at last, and took the pebbly road that wound through the tall grass. I knocked on the door of her farmhouse.

"She left last year," said her mother, without recognizing me. "She's teaching in Bavaria."

I wanted to send her the letters I'd written in the mountains, but I held back in the end. Some evenings, I'd reread them as I did with your notebook, and then one sleepless night, I tore them out along with those I'd written to Barbara. Words could do nothing against walls raised by silence. They spoke only of what no longer existed. Just as well that there should be no trace of them.

We took up our old life, a hard one. We had only half a dozen sheep and three cows. Michael kept us going by starting up Pa's workshop again. The destruction caused by the war was our salvation. Everyone needed tables, chairs, cabinets, benches. Erich would stop by to lend a hand, which meant that during the summer of '45, I was once again the one who tilled the garden and grazed the animals. Once again, I ended up eating bread and cheese by myself in the pastures. I looked at the vast valleys and lazy cows grazing on grass combed by the wind. I felt numb, as if the snow were still at my heels. As if I were still sleeping on decaying leaves. An old ginger-colored dog was wandering around the pasture. He licked my hands and snuggled up next to me. I'd pet his tail, and from time to time pull out some of my food for him. He circled the cows and they obeyed him. I called him Fleck and decided to take him with me. It would do me good to have a little company.

One morning I saw you through the trees. You were still a little girl. I left the animals to the dog and followed you. I called you, but you kept on walking, your steps slow, your back straight. You wore only a T-shirt and your feet were bare. I hurried to follow you, panting as I ran, calling out your name. My hoarse voice got lost amid the rustling of the birches. Though you walked slowly, the distance between us remained. I ran until I was out of breath and, legs trembling, I leaned against a tree. I beat it with my fists, shouting that it was your fault, our misery, Michael's Nazism, the bullets I'd fired at the Germans. You and only you were to blame. For everything. And I went away swearing that I'd throw out your toys. I'd throw the wooden doll Pa made you into the stove.

2

On Sundays Erich went to Mass. Occasionally I'd go with him, and we sat on the pew at the back, where I'd sat years before with Maja and Barbara.

One day he said, "C'mon, get on your bike," and he rode ahead of me to the worksite.

Fleck followed us and when we got there he looked at us with his tongue hanging out of his mouth. You could hear buzzards, the stream, dogs barking. Everything was suffused with sunlight, apart from the thin shadows of the trees. Erich lit a cigarette, and with narrowed eyes he surveyed the artificial barrier, abandoned mines and old shacks with broken boards, which had once been packed with workers.

"Maybe the others were right and they couldn't do it," I said.

"We've been lucky, Trina."

We stood and stared, drawing long sighs. Erich wasn't sure whether to hug me in the middle of all that rubble or remain wary.

"When they take it all away," he pointed to the crane and the mounds of earth, "when they fill up the ditches and I see grass growing again, then we can really forget all about this."

★

Day after day, commissions for furniture came through Michael's workshop and the low prices meant that payments weren't that late. I'd finally started teaching again – there were two schools now in the South Tyrol, one of them Italian, the other German – and my teacher's salary along with the earnings from the carpentry shop allowed us to live a bit better.

Erich said, "As soon as we put a little money away I'll buy some more cows. I'll breed them and we'll have stables full of calves. We'll send the animals back up to the mountain pastures and we'll be able to sell them at the fairs for a good price."

Like everyone else, we'd been drained by the war, but all the same we were ready for the chance to live again. On the days when we felt stronger, we liked to imagine ourselves at home, listening to the rain falling on the roof while we sat warm inside, telling each other stories in front of the majolica stove. With no more worries.

Michael and Erich took care not to argue. Michael continued to mourn the Führer, and during those years he helped several party officials obtain false passports so they could leave for South America. Erich had welcomed him back to the house without making a fuss, and he ate and worked with him. But he had never resumed loving him again. Life was more about ideals than feelings.

One evening Michael brought home a girl from Glorenza. He'd met her through her father, who'd come to have some chairs adjusted. They said they wanted to get married. She would help out with the accounting in the shop as I had done when I was young. She was well brought up, always apologizing before speaking and all of her sentences began with "In my view." Her name was Giovanna.

"We'd like to live in Grandpa and Grandma's farmhouse," Michael said.

"You'll have to ask Ma," I replied hurriedly. I didn't know yet how she was doing or whether she was still living in Sondrio with Peppi.

Michael nodded and in his confident tone he said, "I'll go and see her. I'd like her to come to the wedding."

I thought he was just saying that, but one day he really did go to Sondrio and he took me with him. We stopped at an inn to eat, and he treated me like a queen. He poured wine for me and when I told him it made my head spin, he laughed and poured me some more. It was unreal being there with Michael, at that table next to the wall in a strange inn, in the somber lamplight, which softened as it fell on our bodies. I sat looking at his face, his big liquid eyes those of a sullen youth. We talked about how good the meat was, how nice the place, but other than that, we didn't know what to say to each other. Maybe because what matters, after the war, is to bury, along with the dead, everything we've seen, everything we've done, and get the hell out of there before we ourselves become part of the wreckage. Before fighting the ghosts of war becomes our own last battle. I was happy talking to him about nothing. In any case, even if Michael had been the most nefarious killer, I wouldn't have known what to do except sit at the table across from him and keep eating. And tell him that I, too, had killed.

"You haven't forgiven me, have you?" He moved his plate aside. "I know you don't believe me, but I really would have come to tell you which road to take." Embarrassed, he pushed his slice of cake around on his plate.

I wasn't sure if he was sincere, but truth didn't matter anymore. In fact, it was the last thing that mattered to me. "I was afraid they'd do something awful to you when they discovered we'd fled," I told him.

"They didn't do anything to me, but only because I was a volunteer."

We left the inn, which was now empty. As he sped away, Michael asked if I remembered him picking gentians for me when he was little and gathering them into a bouquet I never knew where to put. He pointed out where the German roadblocks had been, and told me how many soldiers armed with machine guns there had been until a short time ago. He also told me about the partisans he'd caught in the woods of the Comacchio Valleys and about his fellow soldiers, whom the partisans had killed in front of him.

"They wouldn't even give back our friends' bodies," he said, clenching his teeth.

★

Sondrio's Piazza Garibaldi was very busy, and there, too, the faces were those of people who no longer thought about war. If Pa had been alive, he would have felt a sense of peace.

We went round the workshops. Michael would open the glass doors, push me in and let me talk. I'd ask in Italian, "Do you know where the Ponte family lives?"

But there were an infinite number of Pontes in Sondrio, so we walked around for hours.

"Maybe we're not finding them because they're dead," I said, taking his arm.

"You've become just like Pa. You only see the negative side of things," he replied, irritated. He looked straight ahead.

It was dark by the time we stopped looking. Michael said we didn't have time to get back to Curon. He took me to another trattoria, but I only had a cup of hot milk. We talked to the host and asked how it was possible that in all these workshops there could be no one who knew the Pontes.

"What's the name of your brother's wife?" he asked me.

"Irene," I replied.

He wrinkled his forehead, repeated the name to himself, and all at once he hit the counter. "The Pontes you're looking for went to Switzerland. I knew the family well. They fled to Lugano in '44. I don't think they're coming back."

He gave us a room. Michael and I didn't even have our pajamas with us. I was embarrassed to have to sleep in the same bed with him. When we lay down, I thought he'd talk to me about this Giovanna he wanted to marry, whom I'd seen in passing only once. But the moment the light was out he was sleeping like a log.

We left at dawn. When we reached Lugano, an ashen sky was reflected on the calm water of the lake. At the town hall, they told us where the family lived. Ma, her cousin Teresa, Irene, Peppi and a tiny child were packed into a house on the outskirts. A tiny house with a cracked facade. Ma hugged Michael and giggled. "I thought they'd killed you!" She greeted me as if we'd seen each other the day before, just caressing my face. Peppi was the world's most awkward father and the baby, when he fed him, promptly spat his food all over Peppi

We drank some coffee – real coffee, not barley or chicory – and after Michael announced his wedding, Ma took me aside. "Trina, I'm going to stay here. Your brother needs help, my cousin is on her own and it's peaceful here. You two would also do well to leave Curon."

She didn't ask me about life in the mountain huts, about Erich's having deserted, my having shot at Germans. Ma had grown old, with faded eyes and a face as lined as a dry leaf. Yet she still clenched her fists, still fought against letting her thoughts get the better of her.

"They're like claws, thoughts are. Let them go," she used to say while washing clothes at the river, or on evenings when we sat mending late at night.

Curon and the farmhouse were her life, it's true, but Ma was able to detach herself from her memories – even her roots

– just in time, before they imprisoned her. She never got lost, like old people, in tales of another time, and even when she spoke of Pa, it was less like a walk down memory lane and more like scolding him for sneaking off, washing his hands of her, and forcing her to keep going on her own. She really was a free woman, Ma.

Some of Michael's friends came to his wedding, along with Giovanna's cousins and a few people from the other farms. Erich spoke to Giovanna's father throughout the lunch. He said Michael was stubborn but had a big heart. We ate at the inn, and Karl cooked lamb and decanted some old bottles. Giovanna's cousins danced and even made Ma dance a few waltzes. Her eyes shone with tears of joy at the thought of giving the newlyweds her farm.

"If you two don't take it, the mice will," she said, holding their hands.

You could see Curon from the windows of the inn, and it had never looked so beautiful to me. Erich and I were warm again, the war was over and it had spared my small family. It was difficult to believe, but it was all behind us. All I had to do was stop thinking about you.

3

A January day in '46. Freezing fog floating on the air. In the streets, women were coming back from the market, walking against the walls, scarves pulled over their noses. In the fields, the farmers put their hoes down and blew into cupped hands, counting the hours until they could go home and sit down in front of the stove. The news was brought by a fruit seller, who downed a few glasses in Karl's inn before leaving.

We put on our boots and ran to look. Erich marched along, panting, and I stared at the snow. They'd started digging again. About a dozen tractors had arrived, and there were cranes noisily scooping earth into lorries, loading them right up so they could go and dump it on a mound that was growing before our eyes. An immense hole was opening up in front of us, the biggest, deepest ditch I'd ever seen. The levelers were outlining the bed of the canal. Some way off, another hundred laborers who'd suddenly appeared from who knows where were putting up shacks that would serve as storehouses and workshops, canteens and shelters, offices and labs. Everywhere, the air shook with the noise of tools and the rumble of exhaust pipes. Erich urged me to ask the Italians who'd sent them and how long they'd been back at work. I asked whenever they came by, but they'd look up for a second and then go back to their drudgery without answering.

On one side of the site there was a hut with its door open. Inside you could see a table, and on the table, binders and stacks of paper.

"You can't come in here," said a man in German. His hat was pulled down over his eyes and he was chewing a cigar.

"Have the works started up again?"

"Looks like it," he answered sarcastically.

The door banged. Two *carabinieri* ordered us to stay away and not to go beyond the fencing.

On the way home, I kept my eyes on the ground. If the Italian government had sent the workers back to build the dam, then one day the Duce, the war and Hitler would come back too – and the deserter's life, with the snow at our heels. All told, it was pointless to delude yourself that sooner or later you could leave the past behind you. It was destined to remain an open wound.

Erich immediately went round the farms, agitatedly describing what he'd seen. The huge ditch, the hundreds of laborers, the *carabinieri* in front of the hut, cement columns going up. The men told him to leave it: nothing had happened for thirty years. Let the men from the Abruzzo slave away putting down and removing pipes, let the Venetians and Calabrians go on putting in and taking out fences if they felt like it. The old men said that they were old and they were tired, and now it was the young people's turn to roll up their sleeves. But the young people, the few who still lived there, also dismissed the news:

"One more reason to get out of here." So Erich sought out the women. But they too shook their heads, repeating that God wouldn't let it happen, Father Alfred would protect us, that Curon was a bishopric. Only one man, a veteran who was never seen in the piazza, listened to him.

"If they go ahead and build the dam, we'll get out the pistols we took to the front and plant the bombs we learned to make," he said. "The guys from Montecatini had better watch out. The village is full of weapons."

Erich ate supper in silence. While he drank his cup of broth, I asked once more if we could leave this wretched place, where there was just one dictator after another and even without a war, you couldn't live in peace. He scowled at me, lifted his chin and pointed outside the window, as if the reasons that kept him clinging here like ivy had escaped me after all these years.

Exhausted, he threw himself on the bed, hands behind his neck, and started smoking, blowing the smoke toward the ceiling. I leaned against the wall watching him.

"Teach me Italian, Trina. I don't know the words I need to make them listen."

From that day on, we sat at the table every evening after supper writing down our thoughts and lists of words. I read him stories just as I'd read to you, and as I'd told them to Maria. We spoke Italian for hours. When he came back from the pastures and I scrubbed his back in the bath, he forced himself to confide his thoughts in that language. He took his lessons so seriously that if I was distracted, even momentarily, he'd order me to keep going. I made lists of verbs and nouns, I sang him the songs I'd listened to at Barbara's, I taught him sentences he'd already forgotten by morning.

"I can't learn anything," he'd say, slapping his thighs and dropping his head to the table, discouraged.

He was like an old baby, in the grip of his obsessions.

4

Armed with drills and enveloped in clouds of dust, the workers hollowed out tunnels in the space of a few weeks. We no longer saw them bustling about inside the iron fencing. The lorries never stopped coming out of the caves, loaded with stones; others dumped sand. Rows of cement mixers were preparing reinforced concrete that the workers would transform into slabs for building embankments, buttresses, floodgates. Every so often, the man in the hat stopped to exchange a few words with Erich. He'd walk up to him, light his cigar and look over at the mountains. He was Italian, but he spoke fluent German.

"My friend, go back to your wife. We're going to be here for years."

"I want you all to go," Erich said.

The other man gave him a twisted smile and, without taking his eyes from the mountains, blew a few smoke rings.

"Come on in if you want," he said, making for the hut.

Inside it smelled of dust and ink, paper and coffee.

"To stop these works you need the support of people who matter."

"And who are they?" Erich asked, leaning forward. "Who are the people who matter?"

The man in the hat looked around the empty room. He rubbed the head of his cigar against a stone ashtray, and with smoke still in his throat he replied, "Mayors from the other villages, the government in Rome, the bishop, the Pope. You'll have to get all the inhabitants involved. One by one," he concluded, emphasizing each word.

Erich hung his head. "They think you've already tried several times without getting anywhere. They trust in fate, and drag God's protection into it. Many of them don't even know you've come back."

The man in the hat shrugged his shoulders and nodded compassionately. He knew people well; he'd traveled the world his whole life. They were the same everywhere, anxious for peace. Content not to see. That's how it had been when he'd cleared other villages, emptied neighborhoods, demolished houses to put down railway tracks and motorways, thrown cement over fields, built factories along riverbanks. And his work never ran into trouble because it flourished wherever there was blind faith in destiny, absolute trust in God, the heedlessness of men who wanted only peace. All this allowed him to sit there smoking his cigar in his shack while starving yokels recruited in far-off cities arrived on trains to toil away like slaves in the rain, dying of silicosis in underground tunnels. He'd had an easy ride, during his long career, destroying centuries-old squares, houses handed down from father to son, walls that held secrets between husband and wife.

Eventually he said, "It's not too late. But when we get close to the houses, the dam will be ready within a few days. And it'll be the biggest dam in Europe."

The two engineers in jackets and ties came back, the ones who'd paid for the villagers' drinks. They came with some Swiss people. There was a rumor going round that the Swiss were behind the dam, entrepreneurs from Zurich who'd lent tens of millions to Montecatini in order to get it all back in energy, with interest. People in the village began to mutter that it was right to be careful: the Swiss were serious and dangerous people, not like those rogues the Italians. So finally some of them went to the worksite with Erich and saw the thirty-meter-high piles of sand and stones the lorries were moving; demolition teams drilling into the rock; revolving cement mixers; workers putting in turbines and yelling in their incomprehensible dialect, popping out of the tunnels like squirrels from hollow trees. The peasants stood wide-eyed and open-mouthed at the sight of the ditches. They covered their ears with their hands to muffle sounds they'd never heard before.

Day after day the craters continued to spread like an oil stain. The caterpillars and lorries climbed up mountains of earth and it seemed they were perpetually on the verge of tipping over. The workers, like busy ants, merged with one another under the pale winter sunlight. The fields were gone. Their lush expanses had vanished. The earth now vomited only dust, showing off its crushed blue stones; it didn't seem like the same earth in which larches and cyclamen had grown, on which cows and sheep had grazed undisturbed. The still silence of the mountains was buried under the din of machines that never stopped. Not in the evening, and not at night.

One morning Erich succeeded in rounding up about a dozen men. They surrounded the hut of the man in the hat, stamping and shouting. The man in the hat came out, flanked by *carabinieri*. He met Erich's eyes, one side of his mouth tipping up in a smirk. He opened up a map of Resia and Curon. There were red crosses at the corners of the map. It was a large sheet and he had to extend his arm to keep it open. He handed it to a farmer, gesturing to show him that he could turn it around. Some recognized the plan of our village, the woods, the main mountain paths. Others frowned with incomprehension and passed the map to the next person. When the map came back to the man in the hat, he explained that they would be building the dam within the red crosses, but it was a lengthy process requiring continual verification, approval and financing, and it wouldn't impact the village for some time to come. It wasn't even out of the question that they might receive orders blocking the works again.

"We'll have to dig further to reach the inhabited area," he concluded.

Someone asked, "And how high will the water be?"

"Five, maybe ten meters."

The farmers exchanged furtive glances. At that level, Resia and Curon would survive.

"So you're not going to flood the village?"

"No one has ever said we're going to flood it."

As soon as the man in the hat went back in, the *carabinieri* ordered everyone to leave. When the door to the hut closed, the farmers took to the road leading home, dragging their feet through the mud. On the Ortler, the last of the sun couldn't dry the earth.

"The site manager said it'll take years to get to the village."

"Who knows what might happen before then?"

"Hitler and Mussolini could come back."

"They say they're not dead, just hiding in order to regroup."

"If Communism keeps spreading we might become not only Germans or Italians, but perhaps Russians."

"Or Americans, if Communism doesn't spread!"

"And then we'll have to speak American with the Americans, no more German and no more Italian."

"The Americans will build skyscrapers instead of a dam."

"He said they won't flood Curon."

"He said he didn't know."

"All the same, I have my fears."

"You shouldn't."

That's how the farmers bickered, dragging their feet through the mud.

As thousands of workers arrived – olive-skinned boys, most of them stocky with jet-black hair, hungry men who'd left their families thousands of kilometers away, ex-fascists and demobbed soldiers from all over Italy – our young men went north. During the war some of them had gone to Germany, others had hidden in Switzerland, still others had ended up prisoners in Stalin's gulags, and many had taken roads that would not bring them back to the Venosta Valley.

On Saturdays, mothers still came to our house, one at a time, so I could read their letters. But I couldn't lie anymore. Their sons wrote that they didn't want to come back to Curon, where there were only cows and farmers, and no chance to change their lives. When they heard these words, the mothers would put their hands over their faces, but they also said it was true: Curon was a village on the edge of time. Life there was static.

"You don't have any men in your village, only old people," the man in the hat said to Erich one day. "And nothing good comes from old age."

5

With Fleck at his side and a cigarette in his mouth, Erich spent his days watching the lorries come and go, overloaded with soil. He watched, dumbfounded, as the workers built steps to allow underground access and went in there with strange machinery.

"That dam definitely won't be able to flood Curon."

"The Carlino is only a little offshoot of the Adige, a creek, really."

"If they think they're going to fill a ten-meter reservoir with such a small amount of water, it's obvious they can't even calculate."

So they said to Erich, the ones who followed him to the works. But there were others who came to our door and asked what they could do to stop the bastards who'd got it into their heads to ruin us. There was a constant bustle in the house. Erich offered little glasses of grappa and repeated what the man in the hat had said: "We have to write. Barricades aren't enough. We have to ask the people who matter for help."

"But we don't know any people who matter."

"And we don't even know how to write." The farmers spread their hands.

"Father Alfred will write, and Trina can write," Erich replied.

The farmers would then turn and look at me, nodding and frowning.

"Let's write to the mayors of the villages around here, to Italian newspapers and politicians in Rome!"

"We should write to De Gasperi, who was born in Trentino when there was still an empire!" someone interjected.

"And what can the rest of us do?" others asked.

"Keep going to the worksite. They need to know we're keeping an eye on them. Only a few kilometers from here, in Switzerland and in Austria, they tried to build dams but when they ran into opposition from the locals, they let it go."

The commotion placated Erich. He forgot to eat, put his cigarette out before going to bed and kissed my head when I gave him a look for coming home late.

Curon's town hall hired a lawyer from Silandro. The lawyer said that writing a letter to De Gasperi was a good idea, but first it was necessary to obtain a review of the project from the ministry.

"What can I do?" Erich asked.

The lawyer shrugged. "You can't do a thing. It's a political issue."

Erich would come out of his meetings with the lawyer in a terrible mood. To let off steam, he'd go and see Father Alfred, and as long as there was no one else in the church he would sit on a pew and talk to him. He talked to him about worries he hadn't even confessed to me. Some days I envied him his faith, but on others I was afraid that God would disappoint him, too.

"It's odd to see you in church so often," I said. "You never went before."

"Who defended our language when the fascists stamped all over it and imposed their school on us? Who stayed to defend the South Tyrol? The politicians, Italy and Austria fought to wash their hands of us. Only the Church looked out for us."

Father Alfred was worried about the dam too, and he said that as soon as the Bishop of Bressanone came through these parts he would speak to him.

"Let's write to him now!" Erich implored. "We can't wait any longer!"

Father Alfred wrote to him to make Erich happy. And within a few weeks, the bishop did come. At the time, it seemed words could move mountains. The worst mistake was not to question them, not to look for them or let them speak sooner. Words.

Erich and another man set to, along with some of the more pious women from church, dusting the windows and polishing the church furniture. That Sunday, the people thronged the churchyard as they always did when the bishop arrived. Erich and I, however, sat on a pew in the front row. We were so anxious to talk to that huge man, his face so hard it made you drop your gaze. But the bishop celebrated Mass as if we had no priest in the village and hadn't heard Mass for years. He made us pray seated and standing, in German and in

Latin, and when it was finally time for the sermon, he spoke of the afterlife with all the usual fervor, of how horrible or wonderful it might be. It was only at the last that he said, "This village is menaced by a dangerous project. I will write to the Pope to put him in the picture. If we're deserving, his blessed heart will surely help us."

The same night, the man in the hat told Erich they'd decided to raise the water level to fifteen meters.

I was already in bed when he got back. He lay down beside me and rested his hand on my stomach. We no longer made love. The man in the hat had shown him the worksite, taken him down into the tunnels, where workers entered on wagons running on diesel and exited with faces masked in black, as if they'd rubbed coal on their skin. Erich told me how there was no air in there, and the dust made those poor wretches hawk up phlegm constantly, so that they had to take turns going outside in order to catch their breath.

"It's the work of slaves," he told me indignantly, describing workers gone blue in the face while hacking at the ground with pickaxes and cementing the slabs that would one day be washed over by the explosive power of the water.

The workers continued to pour in. Along the roads one ran into endless columns of men climbing toward the village, sacks slung over their shoulders. They looked like barbarian hordes. They camped out in shacks that stretched for twenty-five meters, with a stove in the middle that struggled to heat the space and bunk beds covered with only a bit of straw. These were the same shacks used in prison camps. The man in the hat told Erich that at this point there were a few thousand of them dispersed across the sites nearby. Villages like ours that faced the lake or the banks of the Adige or some other watercourse, but which, unlike Resia and Curon, would not be submerged.

"The industries have cottoned on to the fact that it's a good moment to collect white gold and make stacks of money from it," Erich said through clenched teeth, pulling up the blanket.

I no longer knew what to say to him. I was tired of talking about his battles. The dam didn't mean a thing to me anymore.

"What's wrong?" he asked.

"Nothing," I answered, turning my back to him.

"Why won't you talk?"

"I have nothing to say."

He lay still, hands on his chest.

"Do you still think about Marica?" I asked abruptly.

"I think about her without thinking about her," he answered.

"What does that mean?"

"I can't explain it any other way. I think about her without thinking about her."

"When I get distracted from the thought of her, I feel guilty. You, on the other hand, are so caught up with everything that's happening that you've forgotten her."

"One has to move forward, Trina."

"You're not suffering."

"You talk like an idiot," he shot back.

"You're not suffering over it," I insisted.

He turned suddenly, took my chin in his hands and snapped – so close that I felt his breath on my face – "She's grown up now. If she'd wanted to come back she'd have done so already!"

I lay paralyzed beneath the sheets. His words echoed in the damp silence of the room. He stared at me, full of rage, and then let my chin go as if it were something to be rid of. He curled up, turning his back to me. For the first time, I wondered if he'd turned away from me so I wouldn't see him crying. I was just about asleep when I heard him open the dresser drawer. He took out a small notebook, in the middle of which was a pencil sharpened with a knife, and he started flipping through it in the dark. I switched on the lamp and in its glow I saw some drawings. It was you.

I tried to take the notebook but he grabbed my wrist. He didn't want me to touch it. He drew well, his touch light but more pronounced around the eyes and mouth. Some pages showed only your hands. On one page, the shoes with a bow that I bought for your communion. I saw you bent over the table, doing your homework. In another drawing I was combing your hair. The hair you still wore long, like when you started school.

I didn't know he drew. I didn't know about the notebook hidden under his socks. I didn't really know what he did all the time he was out of the house. After all those years, I knew almost nothing about him.

6

We heard a rumble, as if there'd been an avalanche. I was at school, and I looked out the window for a moment with the children, frozen to the spot. I tried to continue the lessons. When I went out, there were gaggles of people in the street talking excitedly about the dam: there'd been an accident. Concrete tubing had rolled into the ditch, destroying the fencing, overturning a bulldozer and killing someone. I headed for the worksite. I ran, gasping, the sweat streaming down my back. If Erich were dead, I would flee to the mountains and wait for the wolves. I would run to the cave with the German soldiers in it and no matter how long I survived, I would finally look down from the mountaintop at this village I was beginning to detest, with its peasants who barely saw further than their noses and the invading scum who were blatantly lying to us. If this was peace, I preferred the snow and hunger, the nightmare of Nazis breaking down the door.

I ran for hours, short of breath, my heart bursting. I shouted his name through the trees until I was hoarse. There was no one at the site. The ditch was deserted. You could see where the tubing must have crashed, having gathered speed.

The bulldozer's carcass and the tubs for mixing cement and powdered clay were still in the ditch. Some of the workers were wandering around like insects on a hunk of bread. A deathly silence hung over the scene; you could hear the wind breathing over dry earth. I turned toward home, then back toward the worksite, then home again, until I no longer knew where I was. The edge of the forest was only a few steps away. The sun was setting and I couldn't find the right path. The valleys, the village, the roads… I no longer knew them by heart. I was heading for the rows of fir trees when I heard someone call my name. I turned and saw Erich coming toward me, kicking the stones out of his way.

"Are you okay?" I asked breathlessly.

"Wait for me at home next time."

"What happened?"

"Concrete tubing fell from a lorry and rolled into the ditch."

"Is it true that a worker died?"

"More than one. A *carabiniere* died too."

We headed back to the village. In the distance we could see some farmers coming our way. Night had fallen by the time a few drunks clustered around Karl's inn. They drank to spite the dam, the Italian government, the firm of Montecatini, the dead laborers, the *carabinieri*.

"So after this catastrophe, they'll stop the works, isn't that right, Erich Hauser?" the son of the greengrocer needled him.

"I don't know," he answered.

"Of course they'll stop."

"They've already stopped," said another.

"I told you it'd never be built," someone said, and the others nodded.

The works really did stop. The laborers sat on wooden crates in their barracks across from the dam, smoking and catching flies. They passed drinks around and chewed hunks of bread with bovine mouths. Even giving them dirty looks got you nowhere. They were more brutish than our peasants and you could see from their blank looks that the dust had got to their brains and stunted them for ever. As far as they were concerned, it was all one and the same whether they built the dam or sat on wooden crates smoking. They were waiting for Saturday, when they'd form a queue outside the man in the hat's hut, go in and come out with banknotes stuffed in their pockets. They weren't interested in us, in Curon or the valleys. All that mattered was following orders and coughing up the dust that was killing them. No doubt they dreamed at night of their sunny villages and the wives they'd make love to as soon as they got back home.

A small gang of them came to the *carabiniere*'s funeral. After Mass the coffin, draped with the Italian flag, left in a shiny car that took the road to Merano. They'd squeeze the workers in somewhere until Montecatini had carried out the investigation.

The inspectors from Rome established what had happened and filed a report. Meanwhile, the man in the hat moved the workers nearer the Vallelunga road, a flatter area just outside

Curon. He started putting up more shacks there. Prefabs shaped like tiny houses.

"You don't even stop for death?" Erich asked.

The man in the hat opened his hands and frowned.

"What are these hovels for? Are you planning to pen us up in there?"

"If the government doesn't halt the works, those will be temporary lodgings for people who still want to live here," he answered.

"And have you decided to raise the water level some more?"

"It'll be twenty-one meters high."

"Higher than the village."

"Higher than the village," he echoed.

"But the paper hanging on the town hall says you are only going to five meters!" Erich protested. He could barely speak.

"It also says: 'With modifications to the aforementioned project.'"

Day after day, clusters of prefabs rose up like boxes arranged in Indian file. In the evening, the peasants went to peep at them, but the *carabinieri* soon organized patrols and didn't allow anyone to approach. One night, the war veteran who'd been wanting to plant a bomb succeeded in getting into one of the shacks along with two other men. They might have been hoping to blow them up, or maybe just look around. But a gust of wind blew the doors open and the *carabinieri* caught them in the act. They kept them in prison in Glorenza for a couple of days and freed them on Sunday morning, while everyone was coming out of church. When Erich approached to say hello, they shoved him and ordered him to get out of there, as if it were he who'd arrested them. Other men joined in the chorus.

"Get lost!" they chanted. "Drop it, Erich Hauser! Leave us alone!"

I caught up with him. Without a word he headed for home. Following behind, I thought about Barbara. She hadn't spoken to me, not even before leaving for Germany. Our life seemed like a huge mistake.

One day I stood at the window trying to imagine how we'd live in those squalid shacks, when I suddenly had the urge to write. I sat down at the table and stared at the blank page. I wrote that the industries were treating Curon and the valleys like somewhere without a history. That, in fact, we farmed and we raised animals. And before the army of yobs and the horde of engineers had arrived, harmony had reigned between farms and forest, fields and paths. Ours was a rich and peaceful land. To sacrifice all this for a dam was simply uncivilized. A dam can be built somewhere else, but a landscape once destroyed cannot be restored, I concluded. A landscape can't be put right or replicated. That evening I read the page to Erich and he kissed my head. He told me that an action committee had been formed to defend the valley, and they were discussing why the newspapers cared so little for us.

"Italian newspapers, which should take an interest in things Italian. Italy, which they want us to belong to at all costs!" he cried, worked up.

I read my article to him again, and he said, "We'll send this to them as well."

"Yes, but not with my name on it. You sign it."

I soon forgot those words. I didn't ask Erich where they'd ended up, or what was happening with the committee. He continued to stay up late discussing things with Father Alfred, the mayor and the few farmers who cared about the matter, but I didn't want to talk about it anymore. There was too much chaos, and so much card shuffling that you could lose sleep over it. Whenever anyone came and sat by the stove to talk to Erich about what was happening at the worksite, I'd retreat to my room. I was resigned, and the lack of interest I felt matched that of the peasants and their wives. They were right. We couldn't spend all our time thinking about the dam or we'd go crazy. Monitoring the worksite was a Herculean task, which only Erich Hauser could shoulder. Also, the lawyer was slow and he never sent the letter to De Gasperi. In any case it mattered little to De Gasperi that he'd been born under the Austro-Hungarian empire, and it was possible that he didn't even know of Curon's existence. Perhaps he recognized the Venosta Valley as a summer vacation spot and nothing more. I got excited only when Erich asked me to write an article for the German-language newspapers, since the Italian ones didn't mention us or else supported Montecatini's motives, appealing for progress and calling on us to adapt, to share in that progress even though it involved our destruction. I don't know how it came about, but when I sat with a piece of paper in front of me, the words appeared all by themselves, giving form to an anger I didn't know I had, to the jumble of thoughts spinning round in my head. I wasn't afraid to address myself to the bishop or the president of Montecatini or the minister for agriculture, whom the committee invited to our village through one of my letters so he could see what a sacrilege it was to annihilate this valley.

In the space of a few months, Minister Antonio Segni really did come, and the entire time he kept my letter in his pocket. He passed through Sluderno and other nearby villages, stopping in Curon to look at our pastures, our fields, the farmers at work. He informed us that the guys from Montecatini had told him a pack of lies. They'd sworn we were a squalid hamlet already half depopulated, rather than a flourishing village. Father Alfred stood beside him and he never stopped emphasizing in his broken Italian the crimes with which they were staining themselves. All at once the minister went off a few meters, turned his back on us and rubbed his eyes. Turning round again, he began speaking in the tone of someone who's about to make a solemn promise. After Segni uttered a few sentences, his adviser hurriedly seized his arm and shook his head, inviting him to keep quiet. Placing a hand on Father Alfred's shoulder, he spoke instead of Segni.

"The minister will work hard on your behalf, but at this point, we can't guarantee that we'll be able to stop the works. In the unfortunate event that the works should be completed, what we can do is guarantee compensation. You will be adequately recompensed for your losses."

7

One March day we were individually summoned to the judicial tribunal and given a choice: cash compensation or a newly built house.

"But if it's the house," they began, "you'll have to be patient."

"What do you mean, patient?"

"Patient means patient," the staff replied, with the same arrogance as when there was a *podestà*. Fascism was no longer the law, but it was still around all the same, with its arsenal of conceit, high-handedness and all the people Mussolini had brought in, the ones the new Italian Republic needed in order to run its bureaucracy.

Outside the office of the tribunal we looked at each other in astonishment. Once more we had to choose between leaving or waiting. Just like in '39. Those who took the money would go somewhere else, to relatives or some other part of the valley. Those who chose the house were determined to stay, even with water drowning everything.

"So where will the animals graze?"

"And if we sell them, how much will you pay us?"

"How long will we have to stay in those cages?"

"Why is our farm valued at only four lire?"

"Is it true that the official paper stamped with our dispos-session order costs more than a square meter of our fields?"

That's what we shouted at the bespectacled tribunal em-ployees. They, however, replied with irritation that nothing had been decided and they only needed to get an idea of how many houses would have to be built. That we shouldn't force them to call the *carabinieri* to throw us out.

Father Alfred knocked at our door the same day.

"The Pope will receive us!" he announced, holding the bishop's letter. "You're coming to Rome too!" He spoke crisply, more determined than ever.

Erich burst out laughing. He, a farmer from the Venosta Valley, in Rome, with Pius XII! We both laughed. Father Alfred turned serious. "You'll come too," he said again, and he left Erich at the door, arranging to meet him first thing the following morning. Erich left in the Bishop of Bressanone's car and they took the train from Bolzano to Rome. The Pope received them in a private audience. I asked Erich so many times, "What's the Pope like? What did you say to each other? What's his palace like?" But despite our having prepared a brief speech together, he said nothing to the Pope, and Pius XII didn't say a word to him. Erich told me about the Swiss Guard stationed outside the entrance, the frescoed halls, the paintings, the carpets, the vast gardens you could see behind the curtains. He said the Pope was handsome and showed me a photo they'd given him, but the lens had rounded out his face, and he looked bewildered; he didn't exactly seem handsome to me. They'd spoken in Italian during the meeting and Erich didn't have much trouble following the conversation. He'd sat on the edge of a small divan throughout the meeting, watching the Pope nod his head. Even the Bishop of Bressanone had kept quiet. It was, once again, Father Alfred who got the conversation going. Even with Pius XII he waved his bony hands around while speaking and his face went red with anger over the injustice Curon had to endure.

"An injustice that can't leave you unmoved, Holy Father. An injustice that comes after the evil of fascism, from which we were never really liberated. A violence," he went on, his mouth set and his chin jutting forward, "to which we must add the deaths suffered by our population during the conflict, and all the missing who never returned."

The Pope nodded again and asked the three men to pray. But it was only a matter of minutes before he dismissed them, repeating that he would intervene. He would have someone write to the government in Rome to find out from the minister whether it would be possible to review the project.

"Your community is close to my heart," was the last thing he said before he bade them goodbye.

And then once more the corridors, the guards and Rome seen through the car windows, and Erich absorbed in looking at all the palaces and wide streets and thinking about the Pope's face, and the fact that he hadn't even shaken his hand.

"Will he ask God to stop these bastards?" Curon's peasants came to ask.

"He says he cares about our community," Erich responded awkwardly. He didn't know what else to say.

8

Erich asked me to write a letter to the mayors of the neighboring villages. "You cannot pretend that this battle has nothing to do with you. You cannot show yourselves to be indifferent to the danger from the dam. Now that the Pope himself is on our side, encouraging us and advising us to remain united, you must not expect us to do without your support. You must come and protest with us." So I wrote.

Every Sunday, Father Alfred reiterated that we should not leave.

"The first to leave will be declaring Curon and Resia a lost cause," he warned us at the end of every Mass.

People in the village said things were going well. The Pope had taken our case to heart. The committee, the priest, the mayor and Erich Hauser were seeing to everything. There was nothing to do now but wait for the answer from Rome; wait for support to come from the other villages; be patient until the judicial tribunal decided on an amount for our compensation. And who knew? perhaps there would be new accidents in the meantime, or someone would blow up the barracks in Vallelunga – or at least the office of that bastard who always had a cigar in his mouth and a hat over his eyes.

But others said that bombs should be planted in Rome, and in the offices of the Italian newspapers that were ignoring us and supporting Montecatini's interests. I warned Erich not to get involved with people willing to use weapons. But since I didn't trust him, I went to speak to Father Alfred in person.

He got all worked up. "We'd lose the Pope's assistance. We'd lose everyone's support, apart from God's. If that idiot has weapons, tell him not to set a foot in church!" he shouted.

When Erich came home I told him what Father Alfred had said, and he hung his head like a child caught stealing.

The laborers went on working until midnight, even on Sundays. Behind the cobbler's shop you could now see reinforced concrete tubing sticking out of the ground like teeth, and I smelled stagnant water on the air, an odor I'd never caught before. In the distance, other teams were raising embankments and building spillways and floodgates that would soon be opened to let water through, the water that would flood us. We pretended not to see, and we avoided it, trusting the Pope, the committee, Father Alfred. But in the spring of 1947 the dam was behind us, and it never stopped haunting us.

Erich kept himself busy day and night, organizing sit-ins and protests. He assembled small groups that didn't frighten anyone. All it took was a single farmer for him to feel confident, and he could deceive himself into thinking that he mattered.

I went with him whenever I could, afraid he'd find himself alone. Alone with his cries and his impotent rage. I wanted to protect him from being abandoned by the others.

I went with him on that May day, too, when some peasants from Trentino finally joined us in support, and Resia and Curon became for once a single village. Our animals walked beside us, and they bellowed together with us. We showed the *carabinieri*, the laborers, Montecatini's engineers and God everything we had. Our arms, our voice, our animals. Up on the stage, the president of the farmers spoke these words into a megaphone, and I still remember them because they were the ones I wrote for Erich: "The interests of an industrial society are turning against us, against our fields and our houses. Ninety percent of Curon's inhabitants will have to leave their land. Our request is a cry for help. Save us, or we'll be ruined."

The big orange sun warmed his face that afternoon, forcing him to keep his eyes on the papers he gripped between nervous fingers. He was choked up, and when he stopped we clapped and whistled and the cows lowed as if they, too, understood. Finally, the people shouted, they cried, they came into the streets to look each other in the face. Finally the people showed their metal, and on that day at least we weren't thinking only of ourselves, no one was in a hurry to get back indoors, no one had another place they'd rather be because with each man were women, children, animals, the men he'd grown up with, even if they hadn't spoken to him, even if they'd made different choices from his.

Erich pointed out the man in the hat. He was off to one side, without the cigar in his mouth, but with a half-smile. The *carabinieri* were shielding him, but he ignored them. He had the face of someone who's blameless.

9

The ministry sent their reply, and the lawyer from Silandro came to tell us about it.

"They're not going to review anything. The works will proceed," he said dispiritedly. He showed us a sheet of paper we refused to read.

Erich went in search of the man in the hat. He was still in the distant hut with the two *carabinieri*. They were the only ones left.

The man in the hat looked at Erich, stern but compassionate. "They only replied because the Pope asked them to."

"What now?"

"All you can do now is take extreme measures."

Erich opened his gray eyes and sucked in his cigarette smoke while the man in the hat straightened papers on his desk. "Would killing a *carabiniere* or shooting a worker change things?"

"Maybe you should kill me," he said without looking at him.

At school I asked each child to write a letter about why the dam should not be built. At the end of the day I collected them and went to put them up in front of his office. A stack of stories, a bundle of innocence against Montecatini's deception. The man in the hat threw the door open as if I were stationed behind it spying on him. He took the letters in his fat hands and told me to come in; he had some coffee. His table stood between us, cluttered with folders and notebooks. He read a few lines from each letter, his face blank. He refilled my cup.

"Words aren't enough to save you," he said, handing back the bundle of letters. "Not these, nor those that have ended up in the German newspapers under your husband's name."

For the first time, I saw his eyes: black as ink. I wondered to whom he doffed his hat. If he had a woman he regarded through those narrowed eyes.

"Get out of here," he continued, his voice warmer. "Take your animals to another village. You're still young. You can start over."

"My husband will never agree to that."

Other teachers did the same. They left packets of letters. Father Alfred organized collective prayers, processions, vigils. Some farmers, along with people from northern Italy, showed up at the worksite and attempted to cut the chain-link fence. The *carabinieri* arrived immediately to clear them out. A few days later, at the first light of dawn, the same farmers managed to dig under the checkpoint. There were four of them: they threw themselves under the fencing and ran at breakneck speed toward the men working in the ditch.

The *carabinieri* fired into the air, but the same four men ran and threw themselves on the workers like men who were prepared to die. The man in the hat ordered the *carabinieri* not to shoot. There was a brawl, clouds of dust, kicks and punches. There were many laborers and they quickly got the better of the farmers, disarming them and pinning their faces under their boots. Faces red with earth and shame.

From Glorenza reinforcements were sent to the *carabinieri*. There was the same feeling of tension in the streets as during the war. They staked out the roads, and when you crossed the deserted piazza it seemed like a bomb might go off any minute. The only person around was a lanky youth, six foot tall, wrapped in a brown cloak and wearing big, thick glasses. He'd parked his car by the town hall and was walking around with his hands in his coat pockets and his nose in the air. He got as far as the floodgates and looked at the tunnels, which the laborers were covering with earth from the fields. The levelers would go over it, and then they'd plant grass to give the impression that the valley had recovered its long-lost harmony. That the dam had not upset the balance of the land. From time to time he'd stop, pick up some earth and let it fall, sifting it between his fingers. That afternoon he introduced himself to the committee as a Swiss geologist. He'd come to condemn the secrecy with which the inspections had been carried out, and to reveal the existence of entrepreneurs from Zurich backing the project.

"They're the ones who financed Montecatini," he said, getting worked up. "Switzerland doesn't approve of riding roughshod over the will of the people. We wouldn't even consider such methods. And anyhow," he continued, altering his tone, "this soil is composed of dolomite rubble. It doesn't have the least solidity. They can't build a dam on this. You must absolutely demand that they review the project," he concluded, his lenses all steamed up. "The German-language press is on your side. Ask Austria and Switzerland for help, not Italy."

Initially, the committee members regarded him with suspicion, and then they took him to the worksite. Erich knocked at the hut, but when he saw the geologist, the man in the hat turned nasty and he wouldn't let them in. The geologist sneered and again picked up some soil. He said he'd take further surveys and help us publish new articles in the press. He'd send Rome without delay the data that would ensure the failure of the dam and convince everyone on the evidence of his tests.

"If they make it, it will collapse, or there will be an overflow. Or it will never function," he said before leaving.

Father Alfred asked me to write to the Austrian foreign ministry. It was my final letter. "This dam is a danger to you too. Don't forget that this valley was your home for centuries," I concluded.

There was no reply from Vienna. And the geologist with his slouching gait and huge myopic glasses? After that day we never heard from him again.

10

The mayors from the surrounding villages replied. They would not support the request to review the project, nor would they sign any petitions opposing it. When it came down to it, the redirection of the river suited them because it would prevent flooding in their territories.

"What point is there in shooting the man with the hat in the head if not even our neighbors mind if we drown?" Erich asked. He finally handed me the pistols from the German soldiers I'd killed. "You keep them, Trina, before I do something silly."

"Tell me the truth. Is someone planning an attack?"

"I don't know."

"I'm begging you: don't go to the worksite anymore. Go back to the carpentry workshop with your son. Take care of the calves," I said. He held me and put his fingers over my mouth.

It was his way of telling me he couldn't do it.

"Why is it that the closer the end seems, the more desperately attached I feel to the village?" Erich asked me. We were standing that day at the bank of the dam, looking on while Resia's inhabitants were evacuated. They'd suddenly been dispossessed, and we watched them leave their farms in family groups carrying sacks, bags, suitcases. For some inexplicable reason, those who wanted to take their furniture would have had to get employees from Montecatini to do it and pay them I don't remember how many lire. So houses that lost their families remained full of their possessions. The men carried mattresses on their shoulders and the women held babies in their arms and tried to look straight ahead at the clear horizon. Red clouds floated in the sky. Under the inscrutable gaze of the *carabinieri*, Resia's residents walked in single file with the slow step of the condemned, with the pace of those who'd decided to go when faced with dispossession. To Malles, Glorenza and Prato allo Stelvio. Renting, or if they were lucky, staying with siblings, cousins, distant relatives. Father Alfred never took his eyes off those who were leaving the village.

"We are truly lost," he repeated as they walked away.

The families who'd decided to stay headed with heavy legs for the hovels spread over Vallelunga. Narrow, wonky, oblong. Made from a mold. The people from Montecatini had also built us a church that looked like a disused electrical power station. For them, that was providing for our needs.

One morning, a farmer from Curon found half a meter of water in his stables. His chickens were dead and his hay bales had fallen apart and were floating on the water. He went out into the street and started shouting. Everyone rushed from the farms and workshops to their stables and cellars. They all found water. In no time an enraged crowd gathered in the piazza. Erich ran to call Father Alfred. The water was knee-high even in the crypt.

"Those bastards have closed the floodgates without telling us!" Erich exclaimed.

"Let's go to Resia," the priest ordered. "The engineers are in their offices by now."

As soon as Father Alfred arrived, we formed a file. More than two hundred of us. Young and old. Men and women. We marched to Resia. Even Michael went that day. He'd come to see us, one of his usual flying visits with no real point. Since he'd been living in Glorenza and Erich had stopped going to the workshop, we rarely saw each other. Those two had never started talking again.

On the road, some sang in unison, some cried, a few of the women screamed. We got to Resia in the afternoon, and from a distance we saw two Montecatini engineers outside the hut that was serving as a geotechnical laboratory. At first they froze on the spot, but when they saw that we'd formed an army, they quickened their step and ultimately started running like chicken thieves toward a *carabiniere*'s house, calling out his name. The boys at the back left the group in order to follow them. Michael joined them. The rest of us yelled, "Scum!" The kids caught up with the engineers and pushed them toward the crowd, which instantly closed around them. Father Alfred shouted out that no one must dare raise a hand.

"Did you close the floodgates?" The silence was charged.

"We weren't able to inform you," they blundered, out of breath.

He didn't have time to ask anything else before two cars arrived at top speed, screeching to a halt a short distance away from us. The *carabinieri* got out waving pistols in the air and parted the crowd. The engineers ran to hide behind them, and were safely put in one car while many of us continued to insult them. The *carabinieri* then walked purposefully toward Father Alfred, grabbed his wrists and pushed him like a criminal into the second car, which sped off. People yelled and lobbed stones at the cars. Kids sprinted ahead, trying to stop them. Michael yelled, "Shitheads! Fascists!" and he, too, picked up stones.

When the cars disappeared at the end of the road, we stood watching them. Paralyzed. Stunned. Erich and Michael gripped hands for a moment to stop each other from doing anything.

Father Alfred reappeared two days later. They'd thrown him in prison, accused of inciting the people.

During our last months in Curon we felt like we were being killed by water torture. One drop at a time, same spot on the forehead, until the head wears down. I thought back to the fat woman in the mountains encouraging me: "C'mon, we're not dead yet!" but that's all you could say. And then I thought about the engineer who'd ordered the *carabinieri* to beat Erich.

"Progress is worth more than a huddle of houses," he'd said. And effectively, in terms of progress, that's what we were. A huddle of houses.

After the arrest of Father Alfred, we were overwhelmed by resignation, as if someone had put a hand over our eyes. They say the same happens to the terminally ill, those condemned to death, to suicides. Before death, they become calm, infused with a sort of peace whose source is unknown. A feeling of lucidity, with no need for words. I don't know if such resignation is man's greatest pride, his most heroic gesture, the only eternity he can hope for – or if it only confirms his inherent cowardice, given that it's foolish to stop rebelling before the end. I do, however, know something else, something that has nothing to do with this story: if you had come back, not even the thought of being submerged by water would have frightened us. With you, we'd have found the strength to go somewhere else. To start over again at the beginning.

In August they came to mark our houses with crosses. A red cross painted on all the ones they'd blow up with TNT. All that was left of the old village was the little church of Sant'Anna, where New Curon had arisen. They marked our house at dawn. A few minutes later, Ma's, then Anita and Lorenz's house, which the fascists had assigned to Italian immigrants after '39. The last one to leave the village was an old lady with the same name as mine. She yelled from her window that she'd live there standing on the table, and later the roof. They had to remove her by force.

On Sunday we went to sit on the church pew for the last Mass. About ten priests from the Trentino and the Bishop of Bressanone came to perform the service. I didn't listen to it. Too busy trying to reconcile the irreconcilable: God with neglect, God with indifference, God with the misery of the people of Curon, who, as the man in the hat said, were the same as all the other people in the world. Not even the thought of Christ on the cross could appease me, since I continue to believe that it's not worth dying on the cross. Better to hide yourself away; play the tortoise, keep your head in your shell so as not to see the horror outside it.

After Mass, Erich took my hand and we walked along the embankments. A warm sun threw long shadows and made you want to go out into the fields. Our walk seemed just like a walk around the lake, but I had to remember – I could never forget – that it was a dam, and before that, in its place was the field where I used to stretch out with Maja and Barbara, where Michael used to play ball and you ran and ran, not stopping even when Pa called you back.

The bells were sounding in the distance and who knows, maybe when they ring for the last time their tone is different, because that morning it seemed like they were making music that summed up the whole of my life in Curon, a life that had been difficult but bearable because even the most horrible pain, such as your disappearance, was lived alongside your father, and I'd never felt so defeated that I wanted to give up on life. If they'd asked us that day what our greatest wish was, we'd have answered: to continue living in Curon, in that village without a future, which the young had fled and to which so many soldiers had never returned. Just to stay, without knowing anything about what was to come, and with no other certainty. Just to stay.

11

We were still squashed into the barracks when they blew up our farms. The sound of TNT is not like that of bombs. It's a muffled sound, quickly followed by the sound of collapsing walls, cracking foundations, crumbling roofs. Until nothing remains but columns of dust.

We watched the execution from our little hole. Erich held his breath; I crossed my arms. When the first houses were destroyed, I clung to his side, and then watched the rest fall, not even holding my breath. Until the only thing left was the belltower, which the authorities in Rome had given orders to preserve. It took almost a year for the water to cover everything. Slowly, inexorably, it rose halfway up the tower, which from then on looked out over the rippled surface of the water like the torso of a castaway. Before he went to sleep that night, Erich told me that we'd have to go to the bank in Bolzano to get the money we could expect for the farmhouse and the field, but that getting to the city would cost more than the sum we would collect.

Lots of people went away. Out of a hundred families, only about thirty remained. Michael's workshop, too, ended up under water.

For those of us who were staying, Montecatini had put up some communal stables where our animals kicked each other continually. Since the pastures were submerged, Erich decided to take the cows and calves to the butcher. I walked with him down the road that led to San Valentino; the embankment was on one side. Fleck followed behind, whining and exhausted. He was old and walked like a cripple. He constantly whined for us to scratch him and he looked at us with his wintry eyes. The calves moved forward, one after another in single file, looking uncertainly at the water. Behind them came the three cows, with heavy steps and swinging flanks. The sheep came last.

"Take him too," Erich said, pointing to Fleck.

The butcher looked at him, speechless. Erich held out two banknotes. "Please, take him too," he repeated.

I tugged at his arm, begging him not to do it, but he said harshly that it was better this way.

We went home with nothing. The milky sky was coursed by black clouds, the sort that bring summer storms.

I don't know how, but we soon got used to living in thirty-four square meters. That's how much space they allotted to each family, regardless of how many of them there were. I didn't mind the lack of space. Tripping over one another, being forced to look each other in the eye when we fought, looking out the same window was all I wanted. And it was all we had left.

The following year we bought ourselves a television. On Saturdays we invited our neighbors to watch with us so we wouldn't be alone all the time. When Erich went out, I'd leave the radio on, so low that it sounded like groaning. In the background, it helped to distract me from all the usual thoughts I could no longer name.

I kept on going to school, teaching kids how to write, read stories, button aprons. From time to time I would be taken with a little girl. I'd look in her eyes, note how she smiled, and wonder about you. But it happened rarely. Your image escaped me. I couldn't remember the sound of your voice very well. You were like a butterfly on the wing, slow and uncertain, but difficult to capture.

When it rained outside, Erich sat with his elbows on his knees and his face in his hands, looking at the wall. I kept telling him that it was only a question of time, and soon they'd build us a real house, and they'd compensate those who, like us, had lost their work, so we could move forward. That's what they told the town hall, the district, the region. But it was a long time before I got into this two-room apartment they assigned to me. We never received any compensation. Erich never saw this house, because he died three years later in the autumn of '53. He died in his sleep like Pa. The doctor said his heart was bad, but I know it was fatigue that got the better of him. You can die from simple exhaustion. The exhaustion caused by other people, the exhaustion we bring on ourselves, the exhaustion brought about by our ideas. He no longer had his animals, his field had been flooded, he was no longer a farmer, he didn't live in his own village. He was no longer what he wanted to be and life, when you don't recognize it, tires you out in a hurry. Not even God is enough.

The words that come back to me most often are something he said one spring morning when he returned from a walk. The water had suddenly receded and for a few hours the old walls re-emerged, fields of grass and sand. Erich took my hand and led me to the window.

"Today it looks like there's no water anywhere. I can still see the village, the fountain with the cows lining up to drink, the expanse of barley, the fields of grain with Florian, Ludwig and the others scything them."

He said those words to me innocently, and for a moment he seemed once again the boy I used to spy on from behind the door in Pa's house, his blond hair hanging mischievously in his eyes.

After he died, I took the notebook from his jacket, the one he'd shown me that night. Since we no longer had a dresser for our socks, he always carried it around with him. I found new drawings in it. A baby girl on a seesaw, one sleeping in his arms, one riding her bicycle with the wind in her hair. Sometimes I'm not sure the child is you, and I tell myself it's Michael's daughter. Erich wanted to see her and take her for a walk every now and then. He liked being called Grandpa and going with her to throw stones in the water. I don't know if he thought of you then, since by this stage, as he said, he thought of you without thinking of you.

I have nothing left of him apart from the notebook, a

handful of photographs and an old matchbox. I don't even have the hat with the turned-back brim that he always wore when he was young. I put his clothes on a truck that would come by sometimes to pick up clothing and shoes to send on to the poor in other parts of the world. Maybe the only way to go on living is to become someone else, and not settle for staying in the same place. Some days I regret it, but I've been like this my whole life. All of a sudden, I have to get rid of things. Burn them, rip them up, get away from them. I think it's my way of not going crazy.

His grave is behind here, above the old village, in a small cemetery facing the artificial lake. A few days before they blew up the houses, a foreman from Montecatini went to Father Alfred to tell him that they would be tarring over the graveyard. Father Alfred grabbed him by the neck and forced him to kneel by the altar and repeat what he'd said in front of the crucifix. Then he threw him out of the church and ran to call Erich. For the last time, Erich went round all the farms. For the last time, the people gathered in front of the church, even those who'd always slammed the door in his face, to shout that our dead could not be submerged, first by cement and then by water.

We stayed in the piazza until late that night, when the man in the hat got out of the *carabinieri*'s car. In a frosty voice he promised that they'd find a solution. The next day, with masks on their faces, waterproof overalls and pumps of disinfectant across their shoulders, a handful of workers sent by the council disinterred the corpses and transported them up here to New Curon. So that they'd take up less space, the bodies were transferred to small ossuaries and children's caskets. When Father Alfred died many years later, he was buried close to Erich. On his tomb it says *God grant him the joys of heaven*. I didn't have anything written on your father's.

In the summer, I take walks around the artificial lake. The dam generates very little energy. It costs much less to buy it from the nuclear power stations in France. In the space of a few short years, the belltower rising from the still water has become a tourist attraction. Holidaymakers come here, at first amazed, and then barely noticing. They take photos with the belltower in the background, all of them with the same inane smile. As if there weren't any old larch roots under the water or the foundations of our houses, the piazza where we used to gather. As if history did not exist.

Everything has taken on the strange appearance of normality. The geraniums have returned to windowsills and balconies, we've hung cotton curtains at our windows. The houses we live in now look like those of almost any other Alpine hamlet. When holidays are over, you hear an impalpable silence in the streets, which perhaps hides nothing anymore. Even wounds that don't heal sooner or later stop bleeding. Rage, including that caused by violence inflicted on you, will, like everything else, eventually subside and give way to something bigger that I can't name. You'd have to ask the mountains in order to know what it was.

The story of the destruction of our village is summarized in a wooden display case in the car park for tourist buses. There are photos of old Curon, the farms, the farmers with their animals, Father Alfred leading the final procession. You can see Erich in one, with his fellow committee members. They're old black-and-white photos on a glazed bulletin board, with German captions roughly translated into Italian. There's also a little museum that opens now and again for the few interested tourists. There's nothing left of what we once were.

I watch canoes cleaving the water, boats skimming past the belltower, swimmers stretching out to sunbathe. I observe them, forcing myself to understand. No one can know what lies underneath. We can't waste time mourning what was there before us. As Ma used to say, all we can do is move forward. Otherwise God would have put our eyes on the side of our heads. Like fish.

Author's Note

The first time I went to Curon Venosta (Graun im Vinschgau, in German) was a summer's day in 2014. The bus let visitors out in the square, and next to the bus swarms of motorcyclists came and went. A jetty there makes the ideal spot to photograph yourself with the belltower in the background. The queue for taking a selfie is always quite long, and the line of people armed with smartphones was the one image that managed to distract me from the spectacle of the submerged belltower and the water that hides the old villages of Resia and Curon. I can't find anything that more clearly demonstrates the violence of history.

Since that summer, I've returned to Curon several times, and whenever I was away, both the thought and the image of that mountain village on the border between Switzerland and Austria were with me constantly. For a couple of years I studied everything I could, every text and document I found. I asked engineers, historians, sociologists, teachers and librarians for help. Above all, I talked to the witnesses, now elderly, to those years of violence. I wish I could have interviewed someone from Edison, formerly Montecatini, the huge firm that carried out the construction of the dam, but no one ever considered it worth meeting with me or responding to my emails and phone calls. A pity, because it would have been of great interest to consult their archives and ask a few questions. (For example: how and why did twenty-six laborers die during the works? How much attention was given to the social, economic and psychological consequences for the dispossessed? Does the firm accept ethical and moral responsibility for communicating with the population in a language the inhabitants did not understand? Is it true, as reported in the daily paper *Dolomiten* on 7 September 1950, that ten days after Resia and Curon were flooded, Montecatini organized a regatta on the lake?)

I've frequently overlaid the history of Curon with the story of the Alto Adige–South Tyrol, in the knowledge that the dynamics of the village, like those of all small entities, especially those at the border, were sometimes a bit strange. What's more, the history of this region is in my view an episode of Italian history that is not only painful and controversial, but one that still needs to be told, though there are now various texts and novels that talk about it: it is the only place in Europe where fascism and Nazism followed one another without interruption.

To tell the story of the dam I followed the basic sequence of events that emerges from the bibliographies and records, fictionalizing it and only recounting the important episodes. Changes to place names and the order of events and pages of fantasy were obviously needed to meet the demands of the narrative. A novel, after all, cannot do other than falsify and transform. So as is customary, I can state that the characters are invented and any reference to persons or things is purely coincidental. As with certain facts, references to historical characters were necessary (Father Alfred was inspired by Pastor Alfred Rieper, the parish priest of Curon for nearly fifty years), but they don't seem to be substantially undermined despite my having taken certain creative liberties.

It may be the same for many writers, but for me the chronicle of events in the Alto Adige wasn't interesting, nor that of the incidents in one of the many villages crushed by the irresistible political-economic interests of the community at large (which should, after all, be considered with a much wider perspective than that of a novel). Or rather, these things interested me, but only as a starting point. If the history of that region and the dam had not immediately seemed able to accommodate a more intimate and personal story through which to filter History with a capital H; if it hadn't immediately seemed to be of more general value to speak of neglect, of borders, of the abuse of power, of the importance and the impotence of words, regardless of the fascination it exercised on me, I would not have found it sufficiently interesting to study those events or write a novel. I, too, would have stood there, mouth agape at the sight of a belltower that appears to be floating on the water; I would have looked over the jetty to see if I could spy the ruins of that world under the mirror of the lake. And then I, too, would have gone away.

M.B.

Acknowledgments

I'll restrict myself to essential acknowledgments since otherwise the list for this book would be longer than ever. First of all, Alexandra Stecher for her invaluable text *Eingegrenzt und Ausgegrenzt: Heimatverlust und Erinnerungskultur* and for her helpfulness; Elisa Vinco for having helped me to translate from the German more than once; the honorable Albrecht Plangger for having organized a tour of Resia and Curon so that I could meet numerous experts and witnesses; Carlo Romeo for historical consultation and valuable bibliographic suggestions; Professor Letizia Flaim for having introduced me, through her book *Scuole clandestine in Bassa Atesina: 1923–1939* (written with Milena Cossetto) to a considerable bibliography on the clandestine schools. Special thanks go to Florian Eller and, more than anyone, to Ludwig Schöpf, teacher and mine of information on the event, as well as an extraordinary interpreter who allowed me to be in contact with the witnesses and their language. Thanks to my agent, Piergiorgio Nicolazzini, for the tactfulness and attention with which he followed and supported my project. Infinite thanks to the friends who read the novel before publication without holding back on criticism or observations. Particular thanks go to Irene Barichello, Alberto Cipelli, Francesco Pasquale and Stefano Raimondi, who followed the writing of the novel step by step.

Thanks as always to Anna, who knows how to get words out of me I'm not sure I can find.